Acting Edition

MW01068558

DREAM HOU$E

by Eliana Pipes

FOR PRODUCTION INQUIRIES

UNITED STATES AND CANADA
info@concordtheatricals.com
1-866-979-0447

UNITED KINGDOM AND EUROPE
licensing@concordtheatricals.co.uk
020-7054-7298

Each title is subject to availability from Concord Theatricals Corp., depending upon country of performance. Please be aware that *DREAM HOU$E* may not be licensed by Concord Theatricals Corp. in your territory. Professional and amateur producers should contact the nearest Concord Theatricals Corp. office or licensing partner to verify availability.

DREAM HOU$E Co-World Premiere in January 2022, produced by Alliance Theatre, Atlanta, GA, Susan V. Booth, Jennings Hertz Artistic Director, Mike Schleifer, Managing Director. Long Wharf Theatre New Haven, CT, Jacob G. Padrón, Artistic Director, Kit Ingui, Managing Director. Baltimore Center Stage Baltimore, MD Stephanie Ybarra, Artistic Director. The cast was as follows:

ALLIANCE THEATRE:

PATRICIA	Jacqueline Correa
JULIA	Darilyn Castillo
TESSA	Marianna McClellan
THE CREW / ENSEMBLE	Katie Gonzalez, Kenneth Lewis, Blake Lowe, Gabrielle Stephenson, Shelby Woolridge

LONG WHARF THEATRE:

PATRICIA	Renata Eastlick
JULIA	Darilyn Castillo
TESSA	Marianna McClellan
THE CREW / ENSEMBLE	Andrew Martinez, Moira O'Sullivan, Ezra Tozian, Kevin Sisounthone

BALTIMORE CENTER STAGE:

PATRICIA	Renata Eastlick
JULIA	Darilyn Castillo
TESSA	Marianna McClellan
THE CREW / ENSEMBLE	Ricardo Blagrove, Zipporah Brown, Alix Fenhagen, Zak Rosen

CHARACTERS

PATRICIA – Woman, Late 30's, Latina/Afrolatina.

Accountant by day. Julia's older sister, with a distinct Older Sister Complex. She's practical to the core, and a natural caretaker – but often resentful of that role. She lived in the house for over a year taking care of their ailing mother. She believes money brings dignity, security, meaning.

JULIA – Woman. Late 20's, Latina/Afrolatina.

Social studies teacher by day. Patricia's younger sister, six months pregnant. She hasn't lived in the house since she left for college, and is recently reclaiming her heritage in preparation for motherhood. Very sentimental. She believes culture brings dignity, security, meaning.

TESSA – Woman. Early 30's, white.

Real estate agent and TV Host, well-meaning and energetic, always radiating charm. Tessa controls the reality show, and everything within it. She genuinely wants to help the Sisters, and using the show to get them the biggest payout possible is her understanding of what they need.

THE CREW – Any gender, Any ethnicity, (min 2, no max)

A company of actors who make up the ensemble of the piece. The Crew does not speak, but they have choreographed movement. The Crew is a dynamic and near-constant presence on stage, they are the embodied arm of Flip It and List It: both the TV crew, and the renovation crew. They exist on stage in opposition to Sister Space.

SETTING

An old house in a neighborhood called [Hilo Villa], in the process of becoming Hi-Vill.

TIME

Today.

AUTHOR'S NOTE

NOTE ON CASTING

The Latine community is not monolithic and its identities exist along a spectrum of racial, ethnic and cultural backgrounds. The play's themes of displacement are particularly embedded in Indigenous Latine and Black Latine experiences. I encourage producing theaters to be mindful of the communities present in your city. And, as is common in so many families, The Sisters don't need to 'match' or look related.

SISTER SPACE:

There is a combination of light and sound in the play that indicates Sister Space.

Sister Space operates like Twin-Speak or a Shakespearean aside. Either sister can snap them in or out, and they go there in moments of intense emotion. The cameras don't have access, and when they're in Sister Space everyone around them freezes in place.

The idea of a 'snap' into Sister Space indicates the quality of the energetic shift (it is immediate, staccato) but it's not a directive to have the actors snap their fingers (unless you find it helpful).

Sister Space is something that Julia and Patricia share privately at the beginning, but that Tessa gets access to as the play unfolds. Losing the house is something the Sisters agreed to, but losing Sister Space is something they never saw coming.

Snapping in to Sister Space is indicated with **
Leaving Sister Space is indicated with *

SPANISH PRONUNCIATION:

Words in brackets are pronounced in Spanish – example: [Julia] vs. Julia

[Pati] and [Juli] are affectionate nicknames that the sisters use for each other.

Spanish Pronunciation Guide:

Word	English	Spanish
Julia	JOO-Lee-Uh	HU-Lee-Ah
Patricia	Puh-TRISH-Uh	Pa-TREE-See-Ah
Hilo Villa	High-Vill	EE-Loh VEE-Yah

For my Mother, who is my home

Scene One

(A lived-in family home. Clutter, mail, half-empty glasses.)

(On the mantle there's an altar. It can be a religious altar, or simply a familial one with old family photos and spelling bee trophies. It's a place of honor in the house.)

*(**PATRICIA** comes on like a force. She's dressed in professional clothes and constantly checking her watch.)*

(She gets the room in order in one set of flawless motions. She curses and complains under her breath, but her movements are elegant – almost like a dance – the one we all do when company is coming.)

(She levels pictures on the wall, collects every mug in one hand, stuffs envelopes under her arm, uses the hem of her dress to dust the table – until:)

(In one pass, the space is presentable. She smiles. The house looks good. She exits to drop what's in her hands.)

(Then, a rustling. The sound of a door opening.)

*(**JULIA** enters with a large overnight bag and drops it by the door. She's six months*

*pregnant and holds her belly with both
hands, dressed for a picnic in the park.)*

*(She finds herself alone in the house and steps
into the living room to look around, taking
in the space.)*

*(**PATRICIA** returns – she sees the bag, then her
sister. **PATRICIA** stands frozen for a moment,
not sure what to say. **JULIA** notices her and
turns around, excited.)*

JULIA. / Oh, hi! –

PATRICIA. How did you get in?

> *(Beat.)*

JULIA. I had my key.

PATRICIA. Oh, still? –

JULIA. Yeah.

Hi.

> *(**PATRICIA** remembers her manners and
> springs into action.)*

PATRICIA. Hi, hi – it's good to see you!

JULIA. Good to see you too!

PATRICIA. How was the trip over?

JULIA. Eh you know, not too bad, at this hour,

> *(She references her belly.)*

And not to brag or anything, but I only needed *one* pee
break the *entire* time, so –

PATRICIA. Impressive.

*(Awkward beat. They both lock eyes on the overnight bag. **JULIA** moves to put it away, but **PATRICIA** beats her to it.)*

JULIA. Why don't I / put this away –

PATRICIA. Oh here, let me get this bag out of / your way –

JULIA. Oh, I can get it! / It's no problem –

> *(**PATRICIA**'s already gotten it halfway down the hall.)*

PATRICIA. No no no, you're not lifting anything on my watch, don't even think about it.

JULIA. Well – thank you.

PATRICIA. Of course.

> *(**PATRICIA** returns. They take each other in.)*

JULIA. You look good, [Pati]. Really good.

PATRICIA. Oh, thank you.

> *(Pointing to her belly.)*

Well, and you, I mean oh my god! That whole glow thing, you got it.

JULIA. Thanks. She's kicking too. You wanna say hi?

PATRICIA. Can I?

JULIA. Yeah!

> *(**PATRICIA** approaches, and puts her hand on **JULIA**'s stomach. She feels the baby moving.)*

PATRICIA. *Woah*!

JULIA. Right?

PATRICIA. Look at you, you're so much bigger than the last time I saw you.

JULIA. Yeah, the kid's growing fast. I can't get over the house, it looks amazing [Pati], you did such a good job. And the altar! Wait – what happened to those old photos?

PATRICIA. They're fine, I just packed everything up – I wanted to declutter a little.

JULIA. You just don't want anyone to see the braces in your prom picture!

PATRICIA. Not true! But you know what, I remember where I left your sixth grade school picture with the unibrow. Maybe we should pull that one back out?

JULIA. Okay, okay, calm down –

PATRICIA. It looks better this way! That's the point, the [altar] is a place of honor. It shouldn't be too crowded.

JULIA. You're right. It's beautiful.

(She looks around.)

Where's that old grandfather clock? Did you move it?

PATRICIA. Oh, it broke. We had a window replaced and the guys knocked it over and the wood split, glass shattered everywhere, it was a mess – so I had them haul it outside.

JULIA. How could you just throw it away?!

PATRICIA. It was ugly, it didn't even work – and it was cheap, we got it at a garage sale.

JULIA. Well I would've wanted it! Is it still out back? Maybe I can fix it!

PATRICIA. It's too late now, it's been gone for months!

JULIA. Oh. Fine.

*(Beat. **PATRICIA** scoffs.)*

What?

PATRICIA. Look, this is the first time you've been home since Mom –

(Suddenly, the intimate family scene is interrupted.)

*(The **CREW** swarms on from every direction wearing all-black outfits and headsets. They comb through the space in a coordinated operation and adjust the house for the camera, making everything sparkle and adding kitschy "Latin" decor. This is the show's idea of what a Latin home should look like.)*

*(**PATRICIA** takes charge and helps direct the **CREW**, **JULIA** reminisces about what they're moving.)*

Okay, we're starting –

JULIA. Oh woah, so many people –

*(The Sisters fan out and talk to the **CREW**.)*

PATRICIA. Hello! Welcome! Just let me know if you need help finding anything!

JULIA. Um, hi! It's nice to meet you –

*(The **CREW** doesn't respond to her.)*

… No? Okay.

PATRICIA. Do you need a hand? Because I can help if you need – oh alright –

JULIA. Hold on, sorry, where is that going?

PATRICIA. Oh, yes thank you, all of that can go in the hall closet –

JULIA. Where are you taking those? –

(**JULIA** *and* **PATRICIA** *huddle up together.*)

Wait wait wait, [Pati], what's going on?

PATRICIA. Don't worry, this is all part of the plan!

JULIA. Why do they have to take so much away?

PATRICIA. They're just dressing up the house!

JULIA. Yeah but I don't think I've ever seen that before, this isn't our stuff! –

(*A* **CREW** *member approaches the altar.*)

Woah wait!

PATRICIA. Ah, ah – those are a little delicate –

JULIA. That's the altar, careful careful! –

PATRICIA. Oh, this is a little crooked, I can fix it! –

JULIA. That was my favorite one! –

PATRICIA. Oh sorry am I in your way? –

(**PATRICIA** *and* **JULIA** *come back to each other.*)

JULIA. I liked it better before!

PATRICIA. They have their reasons.

JULIA. Yeah I wonder what their *reasons* might be.

PATRICIA. What do you mean?

JULIA. C'mon! You have to admit it is a little... *Colorful.*

PATRICIA. They're just giving it some pop!

JULIA. Yeah it *pops* like the inside of a Taco Bell.

PATRICIA. Don't be rude! Can you just have an open mind about this for like two seconds!

JULIA. ... Is that a donkey?

PATRICIA. Yes... that's a donkey.

> *(Now the set looks like a Macy's display.)*

> *(The **CREW** rushes on again, now they attend to the Sisters and adjust them to be ready for the camera: a cardigan for **JULIA**, a lint roller for **PATRICIA**.)*

Oh, thank you! Sorry, I've been cleaning and it's so dusty –

JULIA. Ah, oh – you think this looks better? Like over the top –?

PATRICIA. Do we need to fix my –?

JULIA. Oh, okay – for sure –

PATRICIA. Soon? Alright –

> *(The last step is attaching a microphone pack to each sister. They notice each other.)*

Thank you. For cooperating with all this.

JULIA. Sure. But, I gotta say, I still do kinda wonder what Mom would / say.

PATRICIA. *(Sharply.)* You have something in your teeth –

JULIA. What?

PATRICIA. In your teeth. Right – right there. Between the front two.

JULIA. Oh – okay. I was tryna make a point that –

PATRICIA. I just figured you'd want to know –

JULIA. No, no – it's fine, I'll get it. Just, she lived here her whole life, you know?

> *(**PATRICIA** is conscious of the **CREW** hovering around them.)*

PATRICIA. Look, I don't want to talk about this right now.

JULIA. I know, but like it's just been on my mind lately
more than I expected –

PATRICIA. [Julia] – / can we just save it?

JULIA. And I think it's worth considering how Mom would
feel about –

>   (**PATRICIA** *snaps them into Sister Space.*)

>   **

>   (*The* **CREW** *freezes in place and lights and
>   sound set the sisters apart.* **PATRICIA** *rounds
>   on* **JULIA**.)

PATRICIA. *Don't* – don't tell me what she would've wanted.

You don't get to do that – okay?

JULIA. Okay. Sorry.

>   (*Beat.* **PATRICIA** *composes herself.*)

PATRICIA. Mom would've wanted what's best for us. Like
always.

JULIA. I know.

PATRICIA. Let's just get ready and do this, alright?

>   (**PATRICIA** *snaps them out of Sister Space.*)

>   *

>   (*The* **CREW** *snaps back into action.*)

>   (*The sisters settle down and get ready.* **JULIA**
>   *tries to dig out the piece of food again, then
>   bares her teeth to her sister.*)

JULIA. Did I get it?

PATRICIA. No, let me do it.

> (**PATRICIA** *uses either her fingers or one of* **JULIA**'s *earrings to dig out the food in her teeth.*)

JULIA. Oh wait wait wait –

PATRICIA. Come on, we don't have much time –

JULIA. *(Mouth full.)* Are your hands clean?

PATRICIA. Don't talk, it makes it harder. Got it!

> (**PATRICIA** *takes her hand out of* **JULIA**'s *mouth, then wipes the food on her sister's arm and laughs when she squirms.*)

JULIA. Ew ew EWW!

PATRICIA. You're such a princess.

JULIA. You're gross.

PATRICIA. But now you look perfect!

Hey, if we wanna get a million bucks, we gotta look like a million bucks, alright?

JULIA. Well right now you're acting like a buck twenty-five.

PATRICIA. *(Swatting at her.)* Tsch! –

JULIA. Ow! You can't hit a pregnant lady.

PATRICIA. You're fine.

> *(Beat.)*

JULIA. You know we're not gonna get that much, right?

PATRICIA. Don't be so negative. It's bad for the baby.

> *(The* **CREW** *leaves. Even as they clear from center stage, their presence is always felt on the periphery. They dart in and out of the*

wings, taking care of the house, setting the scene, and watching the sisters.)

Get ready.

(A huge fanfare – theme song*, lights, energy!)

(TESSA *appears, always bubbly and radiating charm – a cordial queen bee. She's our Host.)*

(She dances in doing a series of overblown poses, as though it was the montage that plays before each episode. A wave, a wink, a handshake, a 'negotiation' pose, a kiss.)

TESSA. Welcome to *Flip it and List It!*

(A crowd screams along with Flip It and List It! *Like* Wheel of Fortune.*)*

Today we're going to get to know the [Castillo] sisters.

They just inherited a gorgeous heritage home in a location that's hot hot hot, and only getting hotter. Their house has great bones, but in its current condition it might not turn many heads in the marketplace.

That's where we come in. Here at Flip it and List It, we believe that with just a few strategic renovations before the open house, these sisters could cash in big at closing.

That's why we give our homeowners a loan to pay for the remodel – courtesy of our generous and faceless investors. But the loan does have some strings attached. Our homeowners are taking a gamble here.

---

* A license to produce DREAM HOU$E does not include a performance license for any third-party or copyrighted music. Licensees should create an original composition or use music in the public domain. For further information, please see Music Use Note on page 3.

If something goes wrong and their house doesn't sell, then they're on the hook for the renovation costs. Bet you don't want to be on the other end of that bill, *yikes!*

But – if they play their cards right, they can earn upgrades and free cash through challenges along the way. *Ka-ching!* One house, two sisters, and everything on the line.

I'm your host, Tessa Westbrook, and this is –

ALL. *Flip It and List It!*

> *(The elaborate light/sound show ends with a crescendo.)*

> *(**PATRICIA** and **JULIA** look at the audience, painfully nervous.)*

TESSA. So! Let's get to know our homeowners!

> *(**TESSA** points to the sisters and the spotlight following her blares onto them. They squint against the light.)*

PATRICIA. Hi, my name's [Patricia].

JULIA. And I'm – [Julia].

TESSA. Great! So tell us a little bit about yourselves ladies!

> *(Beat. They're unprepared.)*

PATRICIA. Umm...

JULIA. Oh, well...

PATRICIA. I, mmm – my... uh... name is Patricia? I already / said that –

> *(**TESSA** drops the presentation and leans in to the sisters.)*

TESSA. Okay! Are we feeling a little camera shy?

PATRICIA. / A little bit, yeah –

JULIA. Definitely, sorry, this is a lot –

TESSA. Oh please, it's okay! It's my fault, really, we just jumped right in there and I didn't give you any time with training wheels –

PATRICIA. It's just a little hard to adjust to the um... the ah...

>   (**PATRICIA** *gestures to the audience.*)

TESSA. The what?

JULIA. I think she means the... uh, that right there...

>   (**JULIA** *gestures to the audience. They all look out.*)

TESSA. Oh! The cameras!

JULIA. Yeah. I kinda feel that too. I mean, I'm cool with it or whatever, but it is a little bit – overw/helming.

PATRICIA. Overwhelming is a great word for it, yeah.

JULIA. And scary.

PATRICIA. Yeah, it's a little scary.

TESSA. Yeah. Just try not to worry about it! You have to treat the cameras like the Crew, just tune them out and eventually you won't notice them at all!

PATRICIA. That's it?

TESSA. Kinda! The secret is to pretend the camera isn't there, but also *never forget* that the camera is there. Does that make sense?

>   (*Beat.*)

JULIA. No not really.

TESSA. It's a balance between seeming very effortless and very prepared – like you're on a job interview or a first date, you know the feeling.

JULIA. *(Laughing.)* Yeah [Patricia], you know what? Just pretend it's like all your dates! You know, all the guys you brought home to meet the family –

PATRICIA. Shhh! Would you stop it!

TESSA. You don't have anything to be worried about, you two are so charming already. Just be yourself, always cheat out for the camera, and smile. They're gonna love you.

PATRICIA. Thank you.

TESSA. Absolutely. And actually, it's pretty important that they do. We've got a big audience and it's crucial that they think you're likeable. Otherwise they'll just tune out.

PATRICIA.	**JULIA**.
Oh.	Weird.

TESSA. Yeah, you know how it is.

And our investors are all about the ad revenue, so – smile big!

> (**JULIA** *takes* **PATRICIA***'s arm and snaps them into Sister Space.* **TESSA** *freezes.)*

> **

JULIA. Wait-wait-wait, I dunno about all this, like –

PATRICIA. What? She's nice! At least she's being real with us.

JULIA. I don't trust her.

PATRICIA. You're being paranoid – she's here to make us money!

JULIA. I dunno [Pati], this feels weird.

PATRICIA. You're just mad because you had to get dressed up. Try to relax, OK?

> (**PATRICIA** *snaps them out of Sister Space.*)

> *

TESSA. So! Let's try it again?

> (*To* **JULIA.**)

So Julia, you're a teacher, isn't that right?

> (*The same setup as the intro before.*)

JULIA. Yes, uh – I teach Social Studies.

TESSA. Ooh, Social Studies! Is that like a fancy word for History?

JULIA. Kind of! It's sort of an interdisciplinary blend: there's some history, some geography, some civics, some sociology.

TESSA. Oh woah, is this a college course?

> (**PATRICIA** *guffaws, then tries to stifle her laughter.* **JULIA** *glares at her, then smiles for the camera.*)

JULIA. Umm, no – it's a charter school, the kids are in the fifth grade. So it's kinda light but, they learn a lot! It's a great job.

TESSA. That sounds wonderful! And looks like you've got a brand new student on the way?

> (**JULIA** *holds her belly and smiles.* **TESSA** *is charming, and it's working on her.*)

JULIA. Yeah, six months along.

TESSA. Congratulations! Wow, it really suits you, you make it look so effortless.

JULIA. Oh, thank you! I've been feeling kinda slow-moving lately.

TESSA. I bet you must be eager to have all this house stuff off your hands then!

JULIA. Well – um –

TESSA. *(To* **PATRICIA**.*)* And Patricia, you work as a nurse, right? What a brave profession.

> *(***PATRICIA*** is thrown.)*

PATRICIA. N-no. I'm not a nurse. I'm an accountant.

TESSA. Oh! I'm so sorry –

PATRICIA. I used to work at a public accounting firm downtown, but uh, I recently transitioned into private practice so –

TESSA. Our team had it down that you were a professional caretaker, our mistake!

PATRICIA. I mean I was caretaking for our Mother for a while, but she – um. She passed away so now I'm an accountant. Or, I was an accountant before too, I'm back to being an accountant, back to *full time*, I mean, um –

> *(Beat, to camera.)*

I do private practice accounting. For individuals and LLC's.

TESSA. Well that's pretty brave too! And you've been living here for the last two years?

PATRICIA. Yes, during the uh – caretaking time. It's a really lovely house.

TESSA. It sure is!

(**TESSA** *roams around the space.*)

So what can you tell me about the house itself.

PATRICIA. Well, as you can see, the house is full of gorgeous original details and a level of craftsmanship that you really can't find anymore. It was built in the 1880's / so the –

JULIA. By our great-great-grandfather!

TESSA. Oh! Wait, really?

PATRICIA. That's the story –

JULIA. Mhm! It was passed down through our mother's side of the family. Our great-great grandfather built this house with his own two hands.

TESSA. Wow! I don't think I knew that about this place, that's incredible!

PATRICIA. And! It's walking distance from two parks, and some lovely boutique shops. The new light rail train takes you directly into the city center, it's very convenient.

JULIA. And our family has lived in this neighborhood for / centuries –

PATRICIA. – Decades.

(*A sore point – they lock eyes with each other, then turn back out and smile for the cameras.*)

Oh, well –

JULIA. Well, I mean / I guess?

PATRICIA. Decades for the two of us, but I guess technically / for the whole –

JULIA. Like a century and a half for the family / the entire family –

PATRICIA. But we're not the entire family just the two of us / on our own –

JULIA. *(Overpowering.)* Years! How's that – years.

PATRICIA. Fine, yes, years!

JULIA. Our family has lived in this town for *years*. And years, and years, and years –

PATRICIA. Alright.

TESSA. Well, Hi-Vill must've been a wonderful place to grow up.

> (**JULIA** *bristles at the term*. **PATRICIA** *knew this was coming.)*

JULIA. Hi-Vill?

PATRICIA. That's – a new nickname. Don't worry about it [Julia]. Should we move on with a tour?

TESSA. Oh, of course! Do you still call it H-hilo –? I'm sorry, I don't want to get it wrong.

JULIA. [Hilo Villa], yes.

TESSA. Oh, that sounds beautiful! [Hilo Villa].

PATRICIA. My sister hasn't lived here for a while, she doesn't know the / abbreviated name.

JULIA. [Hilo Villa] means thread town. Way back when the town was just being founded, this whole region was still segregated, so the farmworkers got edged out of the city and ended up way out here –

PATRICIA. Such a teacher at heart, always got a lesson / in her pocket, okay –

JULIA. We're at a midpoint between the urban industrial center and the agricultural areas in the valley – so the men would go south to farm and manufacture thread, and the women would go north to process and sew it. So, [Hilo Villa].

TESSA. Oh, I see! I wonder why they re-named it.

JULIA. Well, in Spanish the H is silent so Hi-Vill would be the / white –

PATRICIA. – English pronunciation.

TESSA. Hm. I like it the old way. [Hilo Villa]. What a lovely name.

    (Perked up.)

Well, I guess pretty much everything gets abbreviated these days – WeHo, SoHo, SoHa, FenTown, T-Beach. Hard to get around it when the times change.

JULIA. The times haven't changed that much, textiles are still a huge part of our local culture. When I was growing up, there were stands on the side of the road where little old [Abuelitas] would sell these gorgeous handmade traditional dresses. [Oh] they were beautiful, and everyone knew how to sew, I mean *everyone* –

PATRICIA. You don't know how to sew.

JULIA. I had this friend, we called him [Joselito], him and his [manos] would walk all through the [barrio] selling dresses that their [Tía] had made, and one day –

    *(**PATRICIA** rolls her eyes and snaps them into Sister Space:)*

    **

PATRICIA. Okay, come on – what are you doing?

JULIA. What? I'm telling a story, can I get back to it?

PATRICIA. That voice – why do you keep doing that?

    *(A **JULIA** impression.)*

"Oh you know, in our *[barrio]*, *[Joselito]* and his *[Abuelita]*"

JULIA. It's not a voice.

PATRICIA. You don't talk like that – ever! You called [Joselito] Joey since the day you met him!

JULIA. Maybe this place just brings it out of me.

PATRICIA. You sure it isn't for the cameras?

JULIA. Wh – no! How come you're acting like it's a shameful way to talk?

PATRICIA. It's not – but it's not how *you* talk.

JULIA. You're putting on a voice too.

> *(Beat.)*

PATRICIA. No I'm not.

JULIA. Oh yeah?

> *(A **PATRICIA** impression.)*

'Oh yes there are some lovely little *boutiques*, the *craftsmanship* is wonderful, yes this *Vivaldi* is *divine*.'

PATRICIA. I'm a professional woman, this is how I talk now.

JULIA. 'Now!'

PATRICIA. This is my real voice.

JULIA. This is mine.

PATRICIA. Well you sound like a goddamn cartoon.

JULIA. Whatever.

PATRICIA. I don't know what you're trying to prove.

JULIA. That's funny – because I know *exactly* what you're tryna prove.

(**JULIA** *snaps them out of Sister Space.*)

*

(**JULIA** *goes back to her story,* **TESSA** *is rapt.*)

So, every week they came by our block and I wanted one of those dresses *so* badly. I kept imagining how it would feel to twirl and watch that big skirt fan out and spin with me. So I begged my [Mami] to let me get one, and one day –

(**TESSA** *waves. Latin acoustic guitar music begins to play softly*, *underscoring her story.*)

What – what's that?

TESSA. The song? Oh I thought it might be some nice ambiance! To complement your story, you know? I was getting so swept up, keep going – please!

JULIA. Oh, okay sure. I don't think I know this one.

(*She listens, and sways to the music.*)

That's really pretty, actually. Uh – where was I?

TESSA. The dresses.

JULIA. Yes! So! [Joselito] and his brothers used to make me so nervous, because they were like these big tall [macho] boys and I was in like the seventh grade –

(*A* **CREW** *member comes on and tucks a red carnation behind* **JULIA***'s ear. It throws her off.*)

Wait, what was –?

---

* A license to produce DREAM HOU$E does not include a performance license for any third-party or copyrighted music. Licensees should create an original composition or use music in the public domain. For further information, please see Music Use Note on page 3

TESSA. What happened next?

JULIA. Um. Well, they just made me so embarrassed. But I really wanted one of those dresses –

> *(The* **CREW** *adjusts the light to a romantic rosy pink tone, in line with the music. The* **CREW** *comes back on with castanets and streamers, dancing to the Latin score*.)*

> *(The noise is almost deafening, and* **JULIA** *shouts over it.)*

TESSA. Keep going!

JULIA. So, I uh – I got my Mom to agree to let me have one so the next time they came around I waved them down – but then uh. Uh. I – um. It's slipping my mind for some reason.

PATRICIA. I remember!

> *(**PATRICIA** steps forward to spare **JULIA** from the spotlight.)*

> *(As she speaks, she takes the flower out of **JULIA**'s hair and pops it into a vase nearby, completing an arrangement. The music and lights retreat.)*

You were sweating in front of Joey, about to blow all the money to your name on a circle skirt – and then I came running down the stairs to stop you. I'd made you one, as a surprise for your birthday. The stitching was crooked and the ribbon was pink, not red like you wanted. But you looked beautiful.

> (**PATRICIA** *tidies* **JULIA** *up, then she turns to*
> **TESSA**.*)*

How about we give you a tour?

TESSA. Sounds great.

> *(They step through each room. The spaces*
> *aren't fully realized on stage, it should be*
> *something representational.)*

> *(The sisters give the tour tenderly, memories*
> *washing over them. Especially* **JULIA**.*)*

PATRICIA. That big arch over there is the entryway, and it
opens up right here into the living room –

JULIA. Perfect for a grand entrance, makes you feel like a
movie star –

PATRICIA. And the fireplace is still fully functional, really
the heart of the home –

TESSA. I am a sucker for those high ceilings!

JULIA. This was where our mother would sit, right here /
was her chair.

> *(They move into the kitchen.)*

PATRICIA. And the kitchen is over here – the backsplash is
handmade Spanish tiles!

JULIA. It's chipping in some places –

PATRICIA. – but we think it's original!

JULIA. So our great-great grandfather might have made
that too!

TESSA. Gives it sort of a rustic charm, right?

PATRICIA. Absolutely, and it's so spacious – especially for
homes in this area.

JULIA. Yeah, at parties we'd have half the family in here cooking at once, with no trouble.

TESSA. That's lovely. The appliances are a bit dated?

JULIA. Oh yeah, that fridge has been around since I was a baby.

PATRICIA. But it's functional! And – vintage!

TESSA. And through here would be the dining room? Again with those high ceilings, incredible –

(They move into the dining room.)

PATRICIA. Yes, and there's more of that original trim, really makes the space feel special. It's fantastic for entertaining.

JULIA. Oh yeah, our [Abuela] used to host these massive parties with so much food I like couldn't get out of bed for days. It's a great space.

TESSA. That's lovely.

Now, tell me something you *hate* about it.

(Beat.)

JULIA. Excuse me?

TESSA. What do you hate about it? There must be something.

JULIA. No, there isn't –

PATRICIA. Sorry, I'm confused –

TESSA. Well, I mean – you can get a little more negative about the house.

You're not here to sell the place to the camera.

PATRICIA. We're not?

TESSA. No! It's a before and after show, we want to give them a transformation!

You should talk about what you think could be better, then sometimes we can even carry it over into the demolition.

JULIA. Demolition?

TESSA. Renovation.

JULIA. Oh... Huh.

TESSA. I know it can feel sort of tricky to criticize, but there's always room for improvement, right? Let's just jump into it – what's through there?

> *(They move into the master bedroom.)*

PATRICIA. The bedrooms. This is the master suite.

TESSA. Oh yes, the *main* suite.

PATRICIA. Oh? Yes! The main suite. It faces west so it has a wonderful view of the sunset.

Our mother loved the sunsets, till the very end.

> *(Beat.)*

That's not – um. Will you cut that part out, I uh –

TESSA. So what's through there?

PATRICIA. There's a master bath that way,

JULIA. *Main* bath.

PATRICIA. Yes, fine, *main* bath, and the closet is through there.

TESSA. Okay, anything else?

> *(Beat. They can't think of anything. They move to the bedrooms.)*

And what's down this hall here?

PATRICIA. These are the other two bedrooms –

JULIA. Ours. This one was mine and that one was hers. Oh my goodness, I used to wipe so many boogers on that wall.

PATRICIA. I scraped them off so you wouldn't get in trouble. There's a shared bathroom down the hall.

(Beat. **TESSA** *waits for a critique.)*

Uh, you should make this bedroom bigger. It's smaller, and it faces the trash bins. It was mine, I was always jealous that she got the better room.

*(***TESSA** *and* **JULIA** *laugh, but* **PATRICIA** *isn't smiling.)*

TESSA. That's so cute!

JULIA. I was the baby!

PATRICIA. *(Quietly.)* That's why I should've had the better room.

TESSA. Alright ladies, thank you for that tour! How about we move back to the living room and I'll tell you a little more about what I've got planned.

PATRICIA. /Okay!

JULIA. Alright.

(They move into the living room.)

(The renovation tour begins. **TESSA** *is enthusiastic, but she has none of the tenderness the sisters had.)*

(Hearing about the demolition visibly wears on **PATRICIA** *and* **JULIA**, *but they fight to keep their smiles on.)*

TESSA. Scott and his team of rugged handymen will do a full scale teardown of the living space. We'll lose these three central walls to create a completely open concept and improve the first floor flow. Then we'll gut the kitchen and add in all new stainless steel appliances to give the space a more modern, less rustic feel.

In the main bedroom, we'll put in a balcony to make the most of those west-facing windows. Your Mom would've loved that, don't you think?

Then we'll make the bedrooms the same size and add another bath, so there won't be any fighting for the next set of sisters living here. So! There you have it!

>   (**JULIA** *snaps them into Sister Space.*)

>   **

JULIA. Wow –

PATRICIA. I know, / I know –

JULIA. I didn't think it was gonna be so *much* –

PATRICIA. I'm surprised too –

JULIA. Like, that's everything, everything gone –

PATRICIA. Come on, don't forget why we're doing all this –

>   (**PATRICIA** *snaps them out of Sister Space.*)

>   *

TESSA. How's this all sounding ladies?

PATRICIA. Well, I guess it depends.

TESSA. Alright then. Let's talk numbers.

>   (*Dramatic music*.* **PATRICIA** *and* **JULIA** *hold hands.*)

---

* A license to produce DREAM HOU$E does not include a performance license for any third-party or copyrighted music. Licensees should create an original composition or use music in the public domain. For further information, please see Music Use Note on page 3.

So, the big reveal. With Scott's renovations in place, and the current state of the market in Hi-Vill, I would feel confident listing this home at...

(A drumroll.)

2.3 million dollars.

(A still and silent beat. Then, all at once:)

(An extended explosion of joy from the sisters.)

(Shouting, laughing, running, jumping, giddy energy. Everyone gets a kiss, everyone gets a hug, languages intertwine: curses and blessings and blubbering.)

(This is a number that can change their lives.)

(Eventually the celebration simmers down, but the giddy energy still hangs in the air, even **TESSA** *gets swept up.)*

Okay, that was wonderful – but I'm not sure we're gonna be able to use all of that take, I heard a couple no no words in there that the network will *not* allow –

JULIA. I mean, can you / blame me?

PATRICIA. I did one too, I think I did one too – / or a lot, I dunno!

JULIA. Oh my god I'm sweating, look at me, I'm sweating!

TESSA. No no, it's wonderful, I'm so glad you're happy! Just – we're gonna need to get it again.

PATRICIA. Of course, of course – I just um. I need to breathe a little.

TESSA. Absolutely – go ahead, take a minute.

(**TESSA** *steps aside and checks emails on her phone. She absorbs into the* **CREW** *on the periphery of the stage.*)

(**PATRICIA** *composes herself and tidies up, but* **JULIA** *is getting emotional.* **PATRICIA** *notices.*)

PATRICIA. Hey, hey –

JULIA. No, it's good – like. It's good.

PATRICIA. Hormone stuff?

JULIA. No that number! Like – / oh my god –

PATRICIA. I know, it's fantastic –

JULIA. Just, what it could do for the baby –

PATRICIA. And for me!

JULIA. It's wonderful!

PATRICIA. It is!

JULIA. It almost makes me feel like we should stay.

(**PATRICIA** *freezes. Then snaps them in to Sister Space.*)

**

PATRICIA. What?

JULIA. If the house is worth so much, I mean. Shouldn't we stay?

PATRICIA. [Julia], you're not thinking clearly –

JULIA. I'm serious [Patricia]! We haven't agreed yet, not really –

PATRICIA. There's a camera crew in the house! –

JULIA. (*She puts her hand on her belly.*) I know I just – seeing all this again? It's getting to me. This place really is something special, and I don't like thinking that the baby won't remember our family home.

PATRICIA. She'll have a new family home! And hers will be worth a million dollars. Maybe more!

JULIA. That's not the same thing. We rode our scooters down this block, and so did our mother, and *her* mother –

PATRICIA. I don't think mom rode a scooter one day in her life.

JULIA. This neighborhood is our community! I want her to have a connection to her heritage –

PATRICIA. / Oh please –

JULIA. To feel like she's *part* of something, a legacy, I mean our great-great-grandfather built this house with his own two hands!

PATRICIA. *(Set off.)* What do you know about 'our great-great-grandfather who built this house with his own two hands'? Anything? Are you sure he was even real?

Because I'm not. I never really was.

I think that story was just something Grandpa said to his buddies one time and it stuck, maybe somebody lied about it and we've all been retelling that lie over and over.

> *(Beat.)*

That 'connection.' Is that for real? Or is it just something we told ourselves?

JULIA. What difference does it make?

PATRICIA. Then move and tell your baby her great-great-*great* grandfather built *that* place.

JULIA. All I'm saying is if [Hilo Villa] is so valuable now, why should we leave?

PATRICIA. I'm saying, Hi-Vill is *only* valuable if we leave.

> (*Beat.* **PATRICIA** *snaps them out of Sister Space.*)

> *

> (**TESSA** *returns to the sisters.* **JULIA** *is still overwhelmed.*)

TESSA. All good? I think we should get one more take of the intro too, while we're at it.

JULIA. I just – I don't know if I can do this.

PATRICIA. [Julia] please –

JULIA. I'm sorry but all this is bringing some stuff up –

TESSA. Oh, no I absolutely understand.

JULIA. You do?

TESSA. Of course.

JULIA. Well, good. Yeah – because there's a lot to consider.

TESSA. Because of your Mom, right?

> (*Beat.* **JULIA** *looks to* **PATRICIA.** *She softens.*)

Sorry if that's too personal, it's just. I haven't lost either of my parents yet and I can't imagine what you two are going through with all this. Taking care of her, and then losing her, then packing up her house? I mean that can't be easy.

PATRICIA. (*Looking to* **JULIA.**) Yes. Thank you, it's not easy.

TESSA. And selling a house is always a hassle, I mean all the fuss and the paperwork *alone* right?

But trying to do that while you're still *processing* something. It's a lot to handle.

JULIA. You're right, it is a lot.

TESSA. But I'm here to help! The show can support you, we can take all this off your plate!

> *(Confidentially.)*

> Listen – I'm gonna get the *best* price I possibly can for you two, okay? We're gonna get what she deserves, what this house deserves! Whatever it takes, you've got my word.

PATRICIA. Thank you. We're ready to do whatever it takes too. Aren't we?

> *(**JULIA** nods.)*

TESSA. So, one more try! We'll do a clean take of the intro, then we'll fast forward to the big price reveal and just do a slightly less *explosive* realization, okay?

> *(Theme music returns*.)*

> *(Here, **JULIA** and **PATRICIA** say their names in English.)*

PATRICIA. Hi, I'm... Patricia.

JULIA. And I'm – Julia.

> *(As **TESSA** steps forward, the sisters lock eyes.)*

TESSA. And this is *Flip It and List It!* We find run-down rustic homes in promising neighborhoods and flip them into sleek and sellable houses – hopefully to help our homeowners score some big bucks, right ladies?

---

* A license to produce DREAM HOU$E does not include a performance license for any third-party or copyrighted music. Licensees should create an original composition or use music in the public domain. For further information, please see Music Use Note on page 3.

(They remember the audience, then smile and nod.)

Well, I'm glad to say that with Scott's renovations, and the way things are looking in the Hi-Vill market, I would feel confident listing this home at – 2.3 million dollars.

(The sisters take in the number with a breath, then –.)

End of Scene One

Scene Two

(Moving boxes everywhere. The **CREW** *buzzes in the periphery, while the sisters are together at center.)*

*(***PATRICIA*** packs boxes. Her movements are diligent and methodical, but she's in a good mood.)*

*(***JULIA*** sits in front of a box too, moving slowly. She's looking over things and reminiscing instead of packing.)*

PATRICIA. Do you have a stroller yet?

I spent all day looking at strollers, there are so many *types*, do you know about the types?

JULIA. Sorta?

PATRICIA. Well you should check it out, it's amazing. Some of those strollers have better safety ratings than my car – GOD, I can get a new car!

*(***PATRICIA*** notices that **JULIA** isn't excited. Or packing.)*

You think you could pack that one any faster?

JULIA. I'm trying, just – it's hard.

PATRICIA. Are you in pain? Is your back okay?

JULIA. No, yeah – it's just. The memories.

PATRICIA. Then suck it up! Come on, I can't pack the whole house by myself!

*(***JULIA*** starts packing faster, but only for a moment. She's distracted by the **CREW**.)*

JULIA. So – are they? Like? ...Is it on? Are we recording?

PATRICIA. I think they always are. I bet they just want to show us packing boxes, it's not a big deal.

JULIA. I just, I've been wondering – what do you want me to call you? Like – on camera?

[Patricia] or Patricia?

PATRICIA. Oh, I dunno. Whatever, you want I guess, I've been switching.

> (**JULIA** *picks up her tea. She takes a small packet of powder out of her purse and stirs it in to the bright cup.*)

JULIA. I've been switching too. That's why I asked, I just feel weird about it, you know?

PATRICIA. Well, it's nothing new, we do it all the time.

> (*She smells the powder.*)

Yugh, what is that smell?

JULIA. Taro powder! I've been getting into all that stuff, traditional medicine and folk /healing –

PATRICIA. (*Not trying to hear about it.*) / Oh, that's nice –

JULIA. I was looking for something to help with the nausea and I wanted something natural, But then once I dove in, there's so much more to it than I realized –

PATRICIA. / Uh-huh, great –

JULIA. Like in [Curandería] everything gets divided into hot and cold states, and in [Santería], pregnancy is associated with water and the ocean, so there are these –

PATRICIA. Alright! Well – I'm glad you're having fun with your little research project but can you just get back to packing.

JULIA. Yeah, I know you think the spiritual stuff is dumb, but it's not all woo woo palo santo –

PATRICIA. I never said that! It's just not really my thing, that's all.

JULIA. It's important! Those folk remedies are part of our history, we have to learn about it.

Especially for people that history tries to write out, women, queer/people.

*(A shift in **PATRICIA**, her eyes flit to the audience/camera, and the **CREW**. She changes the subject.)*

PATRICIA. So! How's [Santi] adjusting now that you're gonna be a [bruja] bride?

JULIA. [Santi]?

*(**JULIA**'s attention flits to the audience/ camera and **CREW**. She's conscious of being watched.)*

He, um. He doesn't care.

PATRICIA. Really? Well you two should start looking at private schools, this can open a lot of doors!

Do you know what you're gonna do with the money?

JULIA. Haven't really thought about it.

PATRICIA. You haven't thought about it at all?

JULIA. Well we don't have the money yet! What are you gonna do?

PATRICIA. *(She lights up.)* Okay-okay-okay – I have a strategy for the big picture, but when it comes to like, *celebrating* it? I'm gonna take myself shopping, and I'm gonna get a dress. Like, a *gorgeous* dress, like sequins.

JULIA. Sequins?

PATRICIA. Crystals! I dunno – diamonds! The point is I'm gonna look amazing.

Then I'm gonna put everything on, get dressed up, and take myself to the country club.

JULIA. A *country club*? You have got to be joking.

PATRICIA. A lot of the clients I work for are members, apparently there's a lot of perks!

    (JULIA *scoffs.*)

Shh! It's a fantasy! Then – I'm gonna order a steak, best one they have. And when it comes? I'm gonna *send. it. back.*

    (*Beat.*)

JULIA. That's terrible.

PATRICIA. No it's not!

JULIA. Yes it is – it's mean, it's petty. Why do you wanna do that to some poor waiter? You were a waitress in high school, did you like it when people yelled at you?

PATRICIA. I'm not yelling at anybody – it's a hypothetical! And anyway they're used to it, rich people send things back all the time, it's part of having *taste*.

JULIA. We're not gonna be *rich* rich, you know that right? Like – you're not gonna crack the one percent overnight, so you might want to dial it down with this whole country club thing before you go buying / yourself a set of golf clubs –

PATRICIA. What is up with you? Why are you so upset?

JULIA. I'm not upset.

PATRICIA. Okay.

    (*They pack.*)

JULIA. I'm sorry, it's just –

(**TESSA** *enters. Music comes on with her.**)

(*The sisters ready themselves for the camera, they're used to this now (and kind of enjoying it).*)

TESSA. Hello hello hello!

PATRICIA. Good / morning!

JULIA. Hi!

TESSA. How's the packing coming ladies?

PATRICIA. It's going pretty well so far! There's a lot to do / around here –

JULIA. – a whole lot to do –

PATRICIA. – but we've made a decent dent.

TESSA. That's impressive!

(**TESSA** *touches* **PATRICIA**'*s arm with an encouraging nudge, and it lands in* **PATRICIA**. *She holds her own arm to feel the spot where* **TESSA**'*s hand was.*)

JULIA. It's been a real trip, I gotta say.

Going through everything, finding all this stuff from when we were little.

TESSA. Bringing up a lot of memories?

JULIA. Yeah, yeah it is.

TESSA. Well good! Because I've got a little challenge for you two.

---

* A license to produce DREAM HOU$E does not include a performance license for any third-party or copyrighted music. Licensees should create an original composition or use music in the public domain. For further information, please see Music Use Note on page 3.

(Challenge music.*)

*(The **CREW** gives each sister a whiteboard and a marker and corrals them into position.)*

Since packing sent you down memory lane, we thought we'd give you a little memory *game* to test just how much you've held on to. The rules are simple: I'll give you a question, you have five seconds to write down your answer, then tell us what you got! If you're both in agreement, you win! Ready?

JULIA.
Wait, I'm confused about –

PATRICIA.
What happens if we –

TESSA. First question! When she was little, what was Julia's comfort food?

(They write.)

Okay! What was it?

(They both flip their whiteboards.)

JULIA.
Cheese [Quesadilla] from [Rosa's].

PATRICIA.
Cheese [Quesadilla] from [Rosa's].

(Ding!)

TESSA. Very well done!

JULIA. Is that place still open?

PATRICIA. Closed. It's a gym now.

(To camera.)

---

* A license to produce DREAM HOU$E does not include a performance license for any third-party or copyrighted music. Licensees should create an original composition or use music in the public domain. For further information, please see Music Use Note on page 3.

With wonderful amenities and great service.

TESSA. Either way, you win that round!

> (*Suddenly the* **CREW** *swarms on and takes away a stack of their already-packed boxes.*)

PATRICIA. Oh woah, where are those going?

TESSA. Up next! What did Patricia want to be when she grew up?

> (**TESSA** *waits for the timer to count down. For each question, they flip their boards as they answer:*)

Go!

PATRICIA.	**JULIA**.
A lawyer.	A lawyer.

> (*Ding!*)

JULIA. It was a good idea too, she was always judging me.

PATRICIA. Hey –

TESSA. Alright then! Two for two!

> (*The* **CREW** *clears another set of boxes.*)

JULIA. Oh – those are going somewhere safe, right?

TESSA. Here's number three – growing up, what was Patricia's most prized possession?

> (**PATRICIA** *starts writing.* **JULIA** *doesn't know.*)

JULIA. Ah – can I pass? Like, pass on the round?

PATRICIA. / You don't remember?

TESSA. Just take your best guess!

PATRICIA. Think back. I used it *every single day*.

TESSA. – Aaaand!

> (**JULIA** *frantically writes. The timer cues them.*)

JULIA.   **PATRICIA.**
  Her flat iron?   My journal.

> (*Buzz.*)

Dammit.   Seriously?

> (**PATRICIA** *shoots her a dirty look.*)

TESSA. Okay, redemption round, one last shot to win. And this question is special because it's less about the past, and more about the future. What will the baby's name be?

> (*They write.*)

Alright!

PATRICIA.   **JULIA.**
  Ramona [Alvarez].   [Ramona Castillo].

> (*Beat.*)

Wait, what?

JULIA. [Ramona Castillo].

TESSA. Oh! Um, hmm. What should we do with that?

> (**PATRICIA** *snaps into Sister Space.*)

> **

PATRICIA. Why is the baby getting our last name? I thought [Santi] wanted you both to take his?

What's going on, did something happen?

JULIA. [Santi] left! We broke up, okay? He left.

PATRICIA. Oh my god –

JULIA. Just like Dad. But at least he waited till I was eleven, [Santi] couldn't even stick around till the baby was born.

PATRICIA. When did this happen, I mean, did he say why? Or –

JULIA. Can we just drop it please? It's bad enough he's not coming on the show, I don't want to have to explain it to those people, I don't want it on the cameras, none of that –

PATRICIA. Why didn't you tell me? I could've – helped.

JULIA. I dunno – you were going on and on about the future and all this stuff you wanna do. I didn't wanna like, dampen the mood!

PATRICIA. Dampen the –? What are you talking / about?

JULIA. I'm gonna be a single mom, [Pati]! Another [Latina] single mom. How does your little imaginary country club feel about that? That little fantasy isn't fun for me!

PATRICIA. Hey – listen to me. Nobody's gonna look down their nose at you – not ever. Once you have the money you can –

JULIA. Oh my god – stop acting like money solves every problem!

PATRICIA. Well at least money won't run out on you!

(*Beat.*)

I'm sorry. I'm sorry. I know you cared about him.

JULIA. I should've seen it coming. It was such a long engagement. It must've been –

PATRICIA. A year and ten months.

JULIA. Yeah. I can't believe you remembered that.

PATRICIA. You got engaged when I moved in to take care of Mom.

JULIA. Oh. Of course.

PATRICIA. So you're doing all this alone?

JULIA. He's pitching in, but I don't know what I can count on. Everything changed. [Santi] was gonna teach the baby Spanish, take her to the homeland. What do I have to give her? That's why I have to learn –

PATRICIA. No, no I mean – you're <u>paying</u> for everything alone?

JULIA. Oh. Yeah, that too.

PATRICIA. Alright. Say the house goes for 2.3 million – after expenses, call it an even two, split between us – you'd have one million dollars to start your life. Let's go with that.

We can think of it in units, ten units of a hundred thousand dollars each:

Right away, take three units to invest and never touch again – that's your wealth.

Another three units for a downpayment on a new house.

Then one unit for the baby's future – you need a college fund.

After that, take one unit to clear out your debts and get a new car.

Then, the last two units go to living expenses to get you through the next five years.

You'll have to go back to work, you need to keep contributing to your savings – but you'll never be sweating the paycheck, never again. And in twenty years you can retire!

After that, take whatever's left over and get yourself something nice! That's what I'd do.

JULIA. ... When you cut it up like that it's like. You make it sound so small.

PATRICIA. It is small. It's barely enough to make a difference.

At the end of the day, a million dollars is not that much money.

JULIA. What? It's more money than our family has ever had!

PATRICIA. I know. And it's not that much.

> (**JULIA** *falls silent.*)

Come on. Let's finish this.

> (**PATRICIA** *snaps them out of Sister Space.*)

> *

TESSA. Let's give you the win on that round!

> (*Ding ding ding!*)

If you ask me, getting the first name right is really close enough.

> (*The* **CREW** *comes on again, two members move to take their mother's chair, but* **JULIA** *reaches out to stop them.*)

JULIA. Wait, wait – leave this! Leave this one.

> (*The* **CREW** *clears the final set of boxes and furniture in a dancelike assembly line over a*

musical flourish*. A flood of boxes leaves the
space. It suddenly feels very empty.)

TESSA. Congratulations ladies – all your packing is done!

PATRICIA. Thank you!

TESSA. Of course.

(The **CREW** *floods on and prepares for the*
next segment, laying plastic over the floors.
TESSA *sidles up to the sisters to chat.)*

This is so fun, right? Are you guys having a good time?

PATRICIA. Well, it's definitely exciting.

TESSA. I'm having a ball, it's nice to work with homeowners
that actually still like each other.

JULIA. What do you mean?

TESSA. Well, this is sort of a trade secret but, most people
on our show are getting divorced. They'll sell to split
the cash in the settlement, then just pretend they're
still a couple while they're on the show to get our help
with staging.

JULIA. That's juicy.

TESSA. Yeah, but most of my job becomes wrangling
personalities. It takes all the fun out of it, honestly. But
you two! It's different with you.

PATRICIA. Different how?

TESSA. Well, you really deserve it.

JULIA. Deserve...?

TESSA. Our help! Better! More!

---

* A license to produce DREAM HOU$E does not include a performance
license for any third-party or copyrighted music. Licensees should create
an original composition or use music in the public domain. For further
information, please see Music Use Note on page 3

(Leaning in.)

You know, in the final rounds I get a say in casting, and I chose you two because I could just tell, you deserve this. Really, we're not really selling the house here, we're selling a story, and your story is just so uplifting. You two, you're good, honest, hardworking people and that's something everyone can root for. And at the end of the day, when you come out on top, the world will see how happy you are, and they'll be happy too. Knowing everything is right where it should be.

> *(**JULIA** seems unsettled. **PATRICIA** seems inspired. The **CREW** finishes setting up and clears away.)*

(Perking up.) Well! Now that all those boxes are out of the way, let's get on to the main event.

JULIA. Another challenge?

TESSA. Nope, but I think it'll be some serious fun! Come this way!

> *(**TESSA** corrals them towards a wall and produces goggles, helmets and a sledgehammer for the sisters.)*

JULIA. What's – what are these?

TESSA. Alright – today is the start of the renovation phase, and we're gonna put our homeowners to work in the process. Remember, as long as you do your research and you work with adequate safety gear, lending a hand in the demolition phase is the easiest way to save money on your renovation.

> *(To the sisters.)*

So! Who wants to take the first swing!

> *(**JULIA** and **PATRICIA** are frozen still.)*

I promise, it's very therapeutic, just think about that rush hour traffic and then WHAM!

    (Beat.)

Come on now, the walls don't bite.

    (**JULIA** *holds her belly.*)

JULIA. I – I can't, with the –

TESSA. Oh, of course! Okay, Patricia, I guess it's on you. Step right up.

    (**PATRICIA** *steps toward the wall. Her knees shake, she lifts the sledgehammer over her shoulder.*)

    (*In the following sequence,* **JULIA** *snaps in to Sister Space and* **PATRICIA** *snaps out:*)

Are you alright?

    **

JULIA. Don't do it.

PATRICIA. Let me focus.

JULIA. Please, [Pati], you can't –

    *

TESSA. I gotta say, I really do think you'll feel better! Once you just, go for it. Confront it! It's like, letting go *actively* instead of just waiting to feel better. It's like immersion therapy, where if you're afraid of snakes they put you in a pit of snakes! Or, you know what maybe that's a bad example –

    **

JULIA. After this there is no going back.

PATRICIA. There's already no going back.

JULIA. What side of history do you want to be on?

PATRICIA. History?!

    *

TESSA. And look, I know it's um. Charged.

Your family house, all that – I *really* get it, I promise I do.

But you're gonna have to let go at some point.

    **

    *(**JULIA** stands in front of the wall, guarding it with her body.)*

JULIA. Do you know how the settlers took over? They'd just move in. They'd barge in with their guns and plant themselves on the land and say "we live here now, you can either deal with it, move out, or die."

PATRICIA. Stop talking like I'm one of your students –

JULIA. And it never stopped, they'd take one town, then another, and another –

PATRICIA. [Julia], the past is the past!

JULIA. The settlers are coming in to town, [Patricia] – and I don't want to let them turn [Hilo Villa] into Hi-Vill!

PATRICIA. Do you have any idea how lucky we are? We get to <u>choose</u> to go! Everybody else got priced out of their rent, pushed out – we get to make a fucking profit! We own this house, we have the keys, most people never get that!

JULIA. Exactly! We know where we come from – and it's ours, we own it! Most people never get *that*! I'd rather sit right here and let this house rot around me, because it's *mine*.

PATRICIA. Ugh, you sound like a child –

JULIA. Don't act like you don't know what I'm talking about, this house is our heritage!

PATRICIA. Stop! Stop saying heritage that way. I don't understand why having a heritage means I have to be poor!

JULIA. What? You are not poor, you make good money!

PATRICIA. Maybe I want great money! I want earth shattering money! I want a yacht and a country club membership and organic groceries! I want ease, I want luxury – I want a fucking break! I don't want to have to work until my bones grind down to dust like our Mother, and her Mother, and <u>hers</u>. If that's my heritage I say no. I am so sick of making sacrifices, I want it ALL!

> (**PATRICIA** *snaps out of Sister Space.*)

> *

> (**PATRICIA** *picks up the sledgehammer and charges towards the wall.* **JULIA** *moves to stop her.*)

JULIA. Wait wait wait wait WAIT –

> (**PATRICIA** *slams her sledgehammer into the wall, taking down a chunk of drywall.*)

> (*Stillness.* **PATRICIA** *is breathing heavy.*)

> (*Then: fibers that look like strands of thread begin to pour out of the hole in the drywall.*)

> (*The stream starts slow, and then gets steadier, like spools unwinding and pooling on the floor.*)

(It looks like the house is bleeding.)

(Thicker air.)

(They snap into Sister Space.)

**

What's happening?

PATRICIA. I don't know.

TESSA. I don't know either.

> *(***TESSA*** *is in Sister Space with them.**)*

(The Sisters look to each other, horrified. They look around to check that they're still in Sister Space. They are. And so is **TESSA**.*)*

(To the Sisters.) Why are you looking at me like that?

(Blackout.)

Scene Three

*(The house. There are more holes in the wall,
each one of them dripping thread.* **JULIA** *and*
PATRICIA *are visibly distressed.* **TESSA** *seems
strangely exhilarated.)*

*(***THE CREW*** tends to the house in the
background. One comes on and brings* **TESSA**
an iced coffee.)

TESSA. Okay! So! The team figured it out.

PATRICIA. What is it?

TESSA. Mold.

PATRICIA. Oh god –

TESSA. This happens sometimes with old houses, but I've
got to say, I've never seen it like this.

This is very bad.

JULIA. Very?

TESSA. Very *very* bad.

PATRICIA. In terms of?

TESSA. Time, money. Everything.

JULIA. *(Hopeful.)* Does this mean we can't go through
with the sale?

TESSA. Well, we'll have to bring in a specialized crew
to clear it out. We might need to tear down the walls
entirely and rebuild from the ground up. It's a definite
complication.

JULIA. / Wait wait, tear down the whole building?

PATRICIA. Oh no-no-no. Complication how?

TESSA. Well, it all depends on how much this all cuts in to our renovation budget. If we have to do a full removal that could be pricey, and either way we'll have to make a disclosure to any potential buyers, and something like this does not inspire confidence –

(**PATRICIA** *is overtaken with nerves.*)

PATRICIA. What can we do? I can do more demolition, give me the thing –! Or take on the painting, maybe? I can do that! Let me paint!

TESSA. We'll see how bad the budget gets.

PATRICIA. What can I –? How do I help? There has to be something, I can do, I had a plan –

JULIA. Hey, hey – calm down okay.

PATRICIA. Is it even safe to be in here right now? Will she be alright, breathing everything in?

TESSA. Everyone should be fine. We just shouldn't stay here long.

We'll book you both a hotel for the rest of the remodel.

PATRICIA. Oh god, okay, okay – let's think.

JULIA. [Pati] –

(**JULIA** *snaps them into Sister Space.* **TESSA** *comes with.* **PATRICIA** *is too upset to notice, but* **JULIA** *stays hyper-aware of* **TESSA.**)

**

(**TESSA** *notices that the* **CREW** *is frozen in place.*)

TESSA. Hello? Excuse me?

(**TESSA** *waves her hand in front of the* **CREW**
Member's face to check if they can see her, but
they're motionless.)

(**JULIA** *pulls* **PATRICIA** *aside and tries to*
calm her down.)

PATRICIA. What are we gonna do? Without this place we
have / nothing –

JULIA. [Patricia] relax, okay?

PATRICIA. We can't even stay with [Santi]! We'll be out /
on the street!

JULIA. You gotta keep your head on straight –

TESSA. Oh woah! Are they all –??

PATRICIA. We need a plan B, we have to – we have to
figure out / what to do next –

JULIA. All you have to do right now is calm down!

PATRICIA. [Juli] I'm so scared –

JULIA. I am too, but it's not the end of the world, [Pati],
you're okay –

TESSA. Hey guys, so can you see that they're not moving
–?

JULIA.	**PATRICIA.**
Shit, not right now –	Oh my god, oh my god –

TESSA. What?? I'm so confused.

JULIA. Can you just give us a minute?

TESSA. I just don't understand! Why is my crew –? Did
you two do this?

JULIA. Don't worry, it's like – it's not your thing okay!

TESSA. Is this because of the mold?

JULIA. *(To* **TESSA**.*)* No! Or, I dunno – just, just give us a minute!

TESSA. Okay.

JULIA. [Pati], will you breathe with me. Ready? In – and out – In – and out –

(They take a deep breath together. **TESSA** *joins in.)*

TESSA. Jeez, you two got really lucky, huh? –

JULIA. What? Lucky how?

TESSA. Well, if you didn't have our help, and if the neighborhood wasn't so hot right now you'd never be able to get this place off your hands.

JULIA. *(To* **PATRICIA**.*)* Don't listen to her –

(To **TESSA**.*)*

She needs space, just back off, okay?

TESSA. This is just part of the process! In every renovation, every house, when you open things up there's an issue. Honestly, that's what makes the show so entertaining.

PATRICIA. / Excuse me?

JULIA. What the hell is that supposed to mean?!

TESSA. Sorry! I didn't mean to be crass – it's just – it's good TV. Nobody would want to watch this show if everything went perfectly. That's the point, it's about the drama. I just mean you shouldn't feel bad about this or anything! It happens all the time.

*(***PATRICIA*** snaps out of Sister Space, turns to the audience.)*

*

PATRICIA. *(To* **TESSA**.*)* You need to turn the cameras off.

JULIA. [Patricia] –

PATRICIA. I'm serious, turn them off – I don't want them to see me this way –

JULIA. [Patricia], [Pati] relax, you're okay –

PATRICIA. No, NO – this can't all have been for nothing.

JULIA. Look at me. [Mírame.] Look at me.

       (**JULIA** *pulls* **PATRICIA** *away from* **TESSA**.)

       (**TESSA** *goes into a corner and focuses. She clicks her heels, claps her hands, experiments with trying to turn on Sister Space herself.*)

Deep breaths okay? Deep breaths.

       (**JULIA** *waits.*)

       (**PATRICIA** *breathes.*)

Look – all this has me thinking, maybe this is a sign?

PATRICIA. A sign? A sign of what?

JULIA. I just can't shake the feeling that there's something else going on here, something bigger.

       (*Suddenly* – **TESSA** *snaps in to Sister Space herself.*)

       **

TESSA. Ooh!

       (**JULIA** *and* **PATRICIA** *turn to look at her, horrified.*)

JULIA. What are you doing?!

TESSA. Sorry? I wanted to try it, you two made it look so fun. Is this what you were doing when you gave each other that look? Like –

(She does an impression of the look.)

PATRICIA. This is too much, this is too much –

TESSA. Okay! Here, here, I'll bring us back –

> *(**TESSA** snaps them back out again.)*

> *

> *(**TESSA** watches as the **CREW** springs to life again, delighted.)*

/ Oooh, there it goes again! Wow, that is just incredible!

PATRICIA. / Oh my god, oh my god –

JULIA. Stop doing that! Can you just –

> *(Something in the walls catches **JULIA**'s eye, she's rapt.)*

Wait – did you see that?

PATRICIA. What?

JULIA. Right there, in the wall, do you see?

> *(**JULIA** goes to the wall, which is still dripping thread. She reaches into the exposed drywall.)*

PATRICIA. Hey! Hey-hey-hey!

> *(**JULIA** pulls out a small tobacco pipe made of clay.)*

> *(**PATRICIA** pulls **JULIA** back.)*

JULIA. Look!

PATRICIA. What the hell are you doing?

JULIA. Look – look [Pati], look!

> *(JULIA puts the pipe in PATRICIA's hands.*
> *TESSA approaches to get a closer look.)*

TESSA. Oh my goodness.

PATRICIA. It's – a little pipe?

TESSA. That was in the wall?

JULIA. I knew it, I knew it!

> *(JULIA reaches into the walls again. PATRICIA*
> *tries to stop her. TESSA takes the pipe and*
> *studies it.)*

TESSA. *(To Camera.)* Oh, I am so glad we're getting this on camera.

PATRICIA. Come on, think about the baby, it could be toxic!

> *(JULIA takes out a crumpled pile of papers.)*

JULIA. Wait a second, oh my god! Newspapers. And, sheet music! I think these are letters too.

PATRICIA. So what?

TESSA. Are they signed?

JULIA. Yes! Look – I can see their names!

They were real, I knew it! I told you! They were real. It's a sign!

> *(JULIA reaches into the walls again.)*

PATRICIA. That – that doesn't prove anything, you're not / making sense –

JULIA. Come on... come on...

PATRICIA. Are you listening to me?! Stop that!

JULIA. Got one!

*(**JULIA** takes out a small, worn-out Virgin Mary statue. She holds it in her hands and closes her eyes, a wave of relief racks her body – she's clearly affected.)*

Our Lady. The house is giving us gifts – I can feel it! Can't you feel it?

*(**JULIA** hands the statue to **PATRICIA**. **PATRICIA** holds on to it and closes her eyes. She tries to feel something.)*

*(**TESSA** studies the sheet music **JULIA** has pulled out of the wall. She presents the items to the camera.)*

TESSA. This really looks original. Look, you can see some water damage here.

JULIA. All of this, it has to mean something, it has to –

PATRICIA. *(To herself, trying to feel something.)* Come on, come on.

TESSA. I wonder what this song is?

*(**JULIA** dives back into the wall. **PATRICIA** keeps trying to feel something.)*

PATRICIA. *(To herself.)* I don't feel anything.

*(**JULIA** takes out a scrap of cloth, like a veil.)*

JULIA. Look – it's beautiful!

PATRICIA. *(To **JULIA**.)* I don't feel anything! I don't feel anything!

*(**JULIA** ignores her, and dives back into the walls.)*

*(**PATRICIA** puts down the statue and rounds on **TESSA**, who's searching through the newspapers.)*

Did you do this?

TESSA. Excuse me? What do you mean?

PATRICIA. Is this you? Is this part of your little show, just another game?

TESSA. No, of course not! People find things in the walls all the time. It was a superstition!

PATRICIA. What are you trying to do to us?

TESSA. It's true! Usually it's just beer bottles from the builders, but sometimes there are real heirlooms in the walls. In Ireland people put cat skulls in the floorboards below the entryway to ward off spirits! I guess this is just one of those houses.

*(**JULIA** still has her arm in the wall.)*

JULIA. I can feel more – if I can just, reach –

PATRICIA. Stop digging in there, just – put on gloves, something! There could be rats, there could be – [Juli] stop it, please!

JULIA. It's speaking to us, the house is speaking to us.

PATRICIA. No it is not! You heard her, this happens all the time! It's just trash, it's old trash!

JULIA. Can't you see? They heard me – they heard my call!

Our ancestors were thinking of us. They were giving us gifts.

*(**JULIA** pulls out a rattle and holds it to her stomach.)*

*(**PATRICIA** hits a breaking point.)*

PATRICIA. Fine – fine, you want a gift from our ancestors?

> (**PATRICIA** *goes to a cardboard box and takes out a feeding bag, then throws it at* **JULIA***'s feet, hard.*)

> (*She gets increasingly more panicked and breathless with each item she throws.*)

Mom's fucking feeding tube!

JULIA. / Ah –

TESSA. Oh woah woah woah –

PATRICIA. She needed it for the last six months of her life, you visited twice in that stretch, and left before dinner both times –

JULIA. How was I supposed to know those were her last six?! –

> (**PATRICIA** *takes a small journal from the box.*)

PATRICIA. Or this? The notepad where she scratched out her Will, by hand. I took it to the lawyer by myself, and I had to pull over because I was crying so hard I couldn't see straight –

> (**PATRICIA** *throws the journal at* **JULIA***'s feet.*)

JULIA. HEY – stop that! You have to calm down, breathe with me, okay! The cameras –

> (**PATRICIA** *takes an ultrasound out of the box.*)

PATRICIA. Oh, here we go, the ultrasound you sent! She kept it by her bed you know, and every day she'd ask me about you, and I'd have to say 'no [Mami], I don't know how [Julia's] doing, she won't return my calls.' –

JULIA. I didn't mean to – it's just, everything was falling apart and I couldn't / make it work!

> (**PATRICIA** *tosses the frame at her feet.*)

PATRICIA.   *Now* you want to move back to the neighborhood, *now* you want to learn about the house, our history? You didn't have the time of day for us –

JULIA. I'm sorry! I know I wasn't perfect, but I can make up for it –

PATRICIA. GIVE UP [JULIA]! Give up!

You are not some saint to the forgotten past of [Hilo Villa] – you ran away. I know it was a shock to your system, to see your hometown turned into a graveyard – but I had to stay with Mom, and I scrubbed blood out of her sheets and I held her hand while she died.

You wanna float through here with your memories and feel good – but you're not good. You left me alone when I needed my sister more than anyone. And now *my* memories of this place are poison.

So give up. And cash out with me so we can both move on, alright?

> (**PATRICIA** *storms out. Thicker air.*)

> (Then **JULIA** *dives back into the walls looking for more.* **TESSA** *watches.*)

> (*Time passes over the transition as:*)

> (*In a choreographed sequence,* **JULIA** *desperately pulls out the remaining object from the walls – lace and thread tumbles down around her, and she arranges all the objects onto a small table for the audience.*)

(**JULIA** *stands behind the table proudly, it's almost like show and tell day at school,* **JULIA***'s heritage project.*)

JULIA. So – essentially what we have here is a time capsule. It's a window into the past.

There are these local newspapers, dated 1899– and some handwritten letters that my relatives sent to each other with all these details about their lives, the family, what they heard in church that week. There's a tobacco pipe, and this Virgin Mary statue, dominos, a pack of playing cards, some fabric.

But the best part by far – is this.

(*She picks up a photograph.*)

A family portrait. It's dated 1911 and it's labeled, so we get their names, and their faces.

TESSA. That's a real piece of history.

JULIA. Exactly! With *my* family. I never thought I'd be able to really see them, see their faces.

They look like, they look like my mother.

TESSA. And like you?

JULIA. Yeah, they do look like me. This stuff is more than a hundred years old, to find something so well-preserved – a *photograph*? It's like a miracle. And it's a reminder that we've always been here. Standing tall. And see this guy, right here? He's the man who built this house – my great-great grandfather, [Julio Antonio Torres II.]

TESSA. Incredible.

JULIA. He came to [Hilo Villa] to get work as a farmer, and then he built this house so that he could start a family. He had four children, these four right here.

And that one right there? That's my great-grandpa, [Rafael]. He's just a little baby, but that's him.

TESSA. Those cheeks!

JULIA. Yeah! I'm still piecing together the details about the other kids, I don't know much about them yet – but there they are.

(**TESSA** *looks to the audience with a sly grin.*)

TESSA. Do you want to?

JULIA. Excuse me?

TESSA. Do you want to know more about them?

JULIA. I mean, of course I do.

TESSA. Well good! Because I have a little surprise for you!

(**TESSA** *waves and acoustic guitar begins to underscore.**)

Flip It and List It! has decided to use the resources of our show to help you put together your family's history!

JULIA. You? Wait what? –

TESSA. Here it is!

(**TESSA** *dramatically reveals a binder labelled 'Castillo Family History' with photo prints and gaudy decorations.*)

Our faceless investors were *so* moved by what you found here that they decided to hire a team of researchers for the case. They took what we knew from the photograph, your family, and the area, and they got

---

* A license to produce DREAM HOU$E does not include a performance license for any third-party or copyrighted music. Licensees should create an original composition or use music in the public domain. For further information, please see Music Use Note on page 3.

to work compiling this! It's everything we could find from A to Z about your family tree.

JULIA. Really?

(**TESSA** *speaks like she's at show and tell too.*)

TESSA. Are you ready to hear what we learned?

JULIA. Hear it?

TESSA. First of all, your great-great grandfather *didn't* actually build this house after all! His brother did, Osvaldo. Julio moved in around 1890 and started a family, but his brother never had kids, so the house just ended up staying with Julio.

JULIA. Oh. That's surprising. Are you sure about that? Because I really –

TESSA. Fascinating story though, right?

And the kids – well, that one, Luis? During Prohibition, he ran a bootleg liquor operation, and he died in a bar fight when he was just fifteen years old!

JULIA. A bar fight?

TESSA. I know – and, two tragic deaths in one family. That couldn't have been easy.

JULIA. Two? Wait – who's the other one? –

TESSA. You don't know the story?

JULIA. No? Could I just read –?

TESSA. Your great-great uncle was named Jorge, he's that one, right there in the photo. He was killed, and from what we could gather in the newspaper, killed in a fairly public way.

JULIA. Oh my god.

TESSA. I know, just terrible. And, as for your great-grandfather – oh.

But, wait, what am I doing? I'm so sorry, I don't want to presume!

(**TESSA** *waves and cuts off the music.*)

You must know more about your family than any of us do! I'm sure you have so many stories, so please – tell us what you know, and we can just fill in the gaps!

JULIA. I mean I'm not sure I can help with everything –

TESSA. Sure you can! You're the expert!

And you know what – since we're digging into the past, let's try to earn you a little cash!

(*Challenge music plays.**)

JULIA. I'm not doing this for the money.

TESSA. Oh, of course. It's for – the baby, right? And your sister?

JULIA. Fine.

TESSA. Okay, let's start with your Mother's side of the family! Your grandfather Nicasio – what do you remember about him?

JULIA. He was a military man, he served in the army.

(*Ding.*)

TESSA. Yes! He was in the army! Do you know if he volunteered, or if he was drafted?

JULIA. I think he was drafted, or – no, volunteered! But maybe? – Actually, I'm not really sure.

(*Buzzer.*)

---

* A license to produce DREAM HOU$E does not include a performance license for any third-party or copyrighted music. Licensees should create an original composition or use music in the public domain. For further information, please see Music Use Note on page 3.

TESSA. Oh! Okay, can you remember anything about him? Any of his stories?

JULIA. He was, um. I was six years old when he died so some of it is, fuzzier? And I – I got bored, when he would just go on and on. So. I don't remember.

    (Buzzer.)

TESSA. Well, how about his wife, Josefa. What do you know about her?

JULIA. My Mother would always tell me I had her eyes.

    (Buzzer.)

Wait, why is that wrong? It's true, that's what she told me.

TESSA. Of course, and that's so sweet! But we were looking for something a little more *historical*, you know? More meaningful.

JULIA. It means something to me.

TESSA. Do you know anything else about her? Anything at all?

JULIA. I think she was, uh…

    (Buzzer.)

TESSA. Why don't we change gears then! Let's talk about your Father. What do you know about his side of the family?

JULIA. I don't see what that has to do with the house.

TESSA. *(Referencing the binder.)* Oh, it's all here. Do you know the name of the town he grew up in?

JULIA. It was – they – I think they moved around.

    (Buzzer.)

TESSA. Not quite. Do you know why his family decided to leave their country and come here?

JULIA. My father and I weren't very – we didn't talk about things like –

(*Buzzer.*)

TESSA. Do you know why he left Hi-Vill?

JULIA. I'm not answering that –

(*Buzzer.*)

Can you – can you stop that sound!

TESSA. You really don't know?

JULIA. No –

TESSA. Nothing? –

JULIA. No – could I just see the research?

(**JULIA** *reaches for the binder.* **TESSA** *ignores her.*)

TESSA. Okay! Let's do something a little more recent then.

What did you think of this neighborhood when you were growing up?

JULIA. What kind of a question is that?

TESSA. A simple one, I think.

JULIA. It was my home town, I loved it, of course I loved it.

(*Buzzer.*)

(**TESSA** *consults the binder again.*)

TESSA. Mmm – it looks like you always said that you couldn't wait to get out.

JULIA. Well every kid wants to leave the nest. The town wasn't as, it wasn't as / progressive –

TESSA. And in college, when people asked where you were from, you said that your hometown was the one two cities over – why is that?

JULIA. That's – that is not true.

(Buzzer.)

TESSA. When people ask you now, do you tell them the truth about where you grew up?

JULIA. Of course I do!

(Ding!)

TESSA. Hm. Interesting.

JULIA. 'Interesting' – what do you mean 'interesting'?

TESSA. What do you think of the *new* Hi-Vill.

JULIA. I – I don't understand the question.

TESSA. Then I'll rephrase it – where did you get your coffee?

> *(**JULIA** looks down at her brightly colored to-go tea cup nearby. It's the same brand she was drinking earlier.)*

JULIA. This? It's tea, I got it from the place around the corner –

TESSA. The new one, right? The trendy little shop with all the plants and the pink walls. You didn't go to the old local place next door?

> *(**JULIA** notices that members of the **CREW** are holding coffee cups too – but theirs are plain white and branded with the logo of the local shop. They toast to her.)*

JULIA. Look, I get to like a coffee shop, OK? There's a whole lot more to gentrification than just coffee shops – and the only reason I go is that they have this herbal tea / that helps with –

TESSA. Woah woah woah – I'm not judging you, I like the new one better too! See!

> (**TESSA** *holds up her iced coffee from earlier, it's from the same brightly-colored brand.*)

JULIA. Oh.

TESSA. Is that why you like it? Because I do?

JULIA. What –? N-no!

> (*Buzzer.*)

TESSA. Come on [Julia], I've already got the answers. It'll be easier if you're just honest.

Do you like Hi-Vill? Even though it is – *different* from how it was when you grew up. Which one do you like better?

JULIA. I don't, I –

> (*Buzzer.*)

TESSA. Are you different from how you were then? Which version of yourself do you like better?

JULIA. I don't want to play anymore –

> (*Buzzer.*)

TESSA. C'mon – think, win some cash, it's for your family, right?

JULIA. No! Just, give me, let me read it –

> (**JULIA** *tries to wrestle the binder out of* **TESSA**'s *hands. They speak over each other –.*)

TESSA. In fifth grade you told your class that you weren't related to your sister, why were you so ashamed /of her?

JULIA. I wasn't – look, can I / just –?

(Buzzer.)

TESSA. Will your daughter be ashamed of you / someday?

JULIA. I just – give it to me, give / me that –

(Buzzer.)

TESSA. What were your mother's last / words?

JULIA. I don't know!

(Buzzer.)

TESSA. What <u>do</u> you know?

JULIA. JUST LET ME HAVE IT!

> *(**JULIA** pulls the binder hard. It flies out of **TESSA**'s hands. **JULIA** is knocked off balance, and stumbles into the table.)*

> *(She knocks the Virgin Mary statue onto the ground, and it shatters.)*

> *(**JULIA** tries to snap into Sister Space, but finds that she can't. It won't work.)*

> *~

> *~

[Pati]! [Patricia]? Are you there?

> *

TESSA. Patricia left, remember?

(**JULIA** *goes silent and gathers the broken pieces.*)

You really did a wonderful job – I know it was kinda, emotional, but – just. Beautiful stuff. Our audiences are gonna love it, this kind of thing really enriches the show. And it'll help you cash out too, the sponsors are gonna go crazy.

(*Beat.*)

And I know you were sort of, hesitating about selling the house, but now look at all this. If we hadn't opened up the walls, you never would've learned all this history.

(*She references the shattered statue.*)

Even if some of it is a little, bruised up.

(*Beat.*)

And thank you. We need more stories like yours out there. And a real, gritty family history like this? It's the kind of story I've always wanted to tell.

(**TESSA** *leaves her.*)

(**JULIA** *crumbles for a moment, then shakes it off and sits in front of the objects.*)

(*She exits, and returns with candles and sage.*)

(*She puts together a makeshift altar and arranges her offerings around the shattered statue of the Virgin Mary.*)

(*It's long past midnight now, the cameras and the* **CREW** *are all gone off to sleep.* **JULIA** *is alone with the house.*)

(*She begins a ceremony with incredible focus.*)

JULIA. Speak to me.

I ask permission from the spirits of this house and this land

I am here to call on my great-great grandfather, [Julio Antonio Torres II]

I call on the spirits of the four directions, and mother earth and father time to be part of this ceremony.

Speak to me.

I want to take up your place as the defender of this home, protector of this land

(She holds her belly.)

The protector of this family.

I need your memory, your strength, and your wisdom, to guide me on my path. Speak to me.

(She waits for a sign.)

(The air is thick, her focus is intense.)

(But nothing comes.)

Hello? Are you there?

Please? Look, I'm really trying here, and this is the best I've got. So come on. Speak.

Should I go further back?! [Moctezuma]? [Yemayá]?

Or should I be calling out some Spaniard's name?

(Note: references to Moctezuma and Yemayá can be substituted for other figures that the actor feels culturally connected to: others have chosen Ixchel or Ibeyí.)

(She waits.)

(Nothing.)

(An idea. She turns back to her paper and tries to translate the words into Spanish. She attempts the ritual in Spanish with a shaky voice.)

(Note: **JULIA** *can also pull out another piece of paper that has a Google translation of the speech, depending on the actor's comfort with Spanish and translation.)*

Hablame.

Pido permiso a los espíritus de esta casa y de esta tierra.

Estoy aquí para llamar a mi um... grande grande abuelo, Julio Antonio Torres el dos.

Llamo a los espíritus de las cuatro direc-direccions y la madre... La madre... –

(She has a meltdown, and shoves the talismans aside – blowing out the candle and crumpling up her papers.)

(She waits.)

(Then she looks back up – towards her mother's chair.)

Mom? [Mamá]?

It's me, Julia! I mean – [Julia].

I don't know what to do.

Will you speak to me? Can I call on you?

I'm so sorry that I didn't say goodbye.

I miss you.

Mom?

[Mami]?

    (She waits. Nothing.)

    (She breaks and tears into the walls looking for more – something more – anything more. She pulls out chunks of drywall with her bare hands.)

    (Blackout.)

Scene Four

*(The house, as **JULIA** left it, in shambles.)*

*(**PATRICIA** stands alone, pacing and smoothing out her floral dress. She's visibly nervous, and making an effort to calm down.)*

*(**TESSA** is holding a small notebook and wandering through the space, writing up damages.)*

TESSA. Oh boy, this is not looking great, is it?

PATRICIA. No, not really. So your renovation people are working on it?

TESSA. Yes. So the walls will be done. That's a start!

PATRICIA. That's good, that's something.

TESSA. But all of this has really set us back. The open house is coming up soon and there's still a lot to tackle. Clearing the debris, getting the floors laid, tiles done.

And then – well making it look like a home is only half the battle.

We have to make it *feel* like one too.

PATRICIA. Okay, how do we do that?

TESSA. It's complicated.

PATRICIA. Will it be expensive?

TESSA. Where's your sister?

PATRICIA. She's, um – she's not here today. I think she had a doctor's appointment.

TESSA. Of course. I don't mean to pry, but have you two spoken, since –?

PATRICIA. Yes. We're fine.

(To the audience.)

She's just not coming to the house today. Doctor's appointment, for the baby.

TESSA. I see.

Well that might be good – we've been wanting to get a little more footage of you, actually.

PATRICIA. Oh, really? Me?

TESSA. Yeah, to give the audience more of a chance to bond with you.

PATRICIA. Oh, well that's very nice. I, um. What do you want me to say?

Or – is there a clip you want, or a question I should answer?

> (**PATRICIA** *faces camera and composes herself.*)

TESSA. Tell me again why you wanted to sell.

PATRICIA. *(Rehearsed.)* Well, now that our mother passed away – I think it's time to let the place go, and relocate into a neighborhood that's a better fit for my needs.

TESSA. OK. And why do you want to sell with Flip It and List It?

PATRICIA. What do you mean?

TESSA. As opposed to just, finding a listing agent on your own. Do you just want to be on TV?

PATRICIA. Honestly, no not particularly.

TESSA. Then what made you choose us?

PATRICIA. Well, I watch the show, it's great. And I guess I was drawn to your – expertise

(Beat.)

I just thought, if we listed with you – or, with the show, that we might be able to attract a different *level* of buyer.

TESSA. Well, that's true. The investment in the renovation is a real boost.

And, what are you hoping for?

PATRICIA. You mean, in terms of money?

TESSA. In terms of selling. Beyond the blurb, I mean. What do you really want?

(*Beat.*)

PATRICIA. (*Sincerely.*) I guess. I guess I want to sell the house because – because I'm hoping for a new chapter.

TESSA. Great, that was a perfect take. Wow.

PATRICIA. Oh, good!

(**TESSA** *speaks to her confidentially.*)

TESSA. You know, I think we have a lot in common.

PATRICIA. You do?

TESSA. I do. I know what it's like to be the person who runs the show – and it's clear that you run the show around here. Except, I get a lot of help running mine.

PATRICIA. Oh, thank you. It's not so bad. And hey, soon enough I'll be a big budget operation.

TESSA. You know how to put on a show too.

PATRICIA. What do you mean?

TESSA. Well for one thing, that tour you gave on our first shooting day? I've never seen a homeowner point out the turn-of-the-century ceiling trim before.

PATRICIA. (*Bashful.*) Well, I mean, I do watch a lot of home improvement shows, it's a guilty pleasure thing.

TESSA. No, it was perfect – I felt like you were hosting the show.

PATRICIA. Well, it would be hard to steal your spotlight.

> *(***TESSA*** *laughs.* ***PATRICIA*** *can't take her eyes off her. Then* ***TESSA*** *looks down at* ***PATRICIA****'s bracelet.)*

TESSA. I like your bracelet.

PATRICIA. Oh, thank you.

> *(***PATRICIA*** *waits for* ***TESSA*** *to move on with the interview, but she doesn't.* ***TESSA*** *looks at the bracelet the way that* ***PATRICIA*** *looked at* ***TESSA****.)*

Well, I had a question actually, about the remodeling timeline prior to the open house –

TESSA. How much did it run you?

PATRICIA. Sorry?

TESSA. The bracelet.

PATRICIA. Oh, I don't remember, actually. It's pretty old, I think it was a gift.

> *(***TESSA*** *starts wandering around the house again. Taking quicker and more copious notes.)*

I think it has a lot of potential. The house.

TESSA. I love the word potential.

PATRICIA. I do too.

> *(***TESSA*** *turns to* ***PATRICIA****.)*

TESSA. Would you sell it to me?

PATRICIA. Sell you – the house?

TESSA. Your bracelet.

> (*Beat.* **PATRICIA** *is skeptical, but intrigued. She holds her own, ready to negotiate.*)

PATRICIA. This?

TESSA. Yes.

PATRICIA. I mean, uh – it's a little beaten up.

TESSA. So let me take it off your hands!

PATRICIA. Is this some kind of test?

TESSA. Why would I test you?

PATRICIA. I just don't understand –

TESSA. Don't get nervous.

PATRICIA. No, I'm not nervous, I just don't see the point.

TESSA. What is it worth, two dollars? I'll give you ten, you can go buy yourself a new one.

Five new ones.

PATRICIA. It's dirty. It's all tarnished and gray.

TESSA. Then why not, right?

> (*Beat.*)

C'mon, are you really gonna miss it?

> (**TESSA** *takes out a bill and holds it up.*)

What do you say?

PATRICIA. How about fifty.

TESSA. Done.

> (*A beat.* **TESSA** *takes out another bill.* **PATRICIA** *works the bracelet off her wrist and hands the bracelet to* **TESSA**.)

(Ding! **PATRICIA** *hears it.)*

PATRICIA. So it <u>was</u> a test?

TESSA. Not a test. A game. And you won!

PATRICIA. I did?

*(****TESSA**** puts the bracelet onto her wrist.)*

TESSA. It fits! Like a charm. Mm, wonderful.

PATRICIA. Good. So!

TESSA. Where were we?

PATRICIA. The house.

TESSA. Yes! Of course, the house!

*(****TESSA**** looks around the space again.* **PATRICIA** *rubs the spot on her wrist where the bracelet used to be.)*

You know, it's old – but it really does have some charm.

Like you were saying, potential. And this area right now? – well, I'm sure you know.

PATRICIA. I do.

TESSA. It's a very very good time to sell.

PATRICIA. That's the plan.

*(****PATRICIA**** smooths out a wrinkle in her dress.)*

TESSA. You look amazing in that dress by the way.

PATRICIA. Oh, thank you!

TESSA. How much do you want for it?

(Beat.)

PATRICIA. I – um, it's not for sale.

TESSA. Then up-sell me. Go ahead.

PATRICIA. Is there anything else you want to ask me about the house? Let's go to the basement, I don't think we've been down there yet, you can see the pipes –

TESSA. I want to discuss the dress.

PATRICIA. I just, I thought this was going to be a more formal sort of interview – can we – move on?

TESSA. A hundred? –

PATRICIA. Why don't we just stick to business –

TESSA. This is business, two hundred? –

PATRICIA. I want to work out the deal, that's all –

TESSA. Three hundred, how's that –

PATRICIA. I just want to talk about the house okay –

TESSA. Don't be stupid, I'm letting you name your price / here –

PATRICIA. *(An outburst.)* Five hundred.

> *(Ding!)*

> *(Silence.)*

> (**TESSA** *smiles and counts out five hundred dollars.*)

> (**PATRICIA** *realizes what she's agreed to. Slowly, she pulls off her dress. She's nearly naked now, with only her undergarments on underneath: a slip, or spanx. She's conscious of the cameras the whole time.*)

> (*She hands the dress to* **TESSA** *and takes the money. She has no pockets, so she holds it in her fists.*)

(**TESSA** *holds the dress close, and drapes it over her shoulders like a mink stole. She loves it.*)

TESSA. I can smell your perfume.

PATRICIA. Can I buy something from you?

TESSA. What do you want?

PATRICIA. I don't know.

TESSA. You don't want anything? Nothing at all? I find that a little hard to believe.

Think. What do you want?

PATRICIA. Nothing that I could really take from you.

(**TESSA** *points to* **PATRICIA**'s *face.*)

TESSA. I want those.

(**PATRICIA** *puts her hands up to her lips.*)

PATRICIA. You want to kiss me?

TESSA. I said, I want those.

PATRICIA. My? You can't buy my lips – or, I mean. I can't give them to you.

TESSA. Your teeth.

(*Beat.*)

PATRICIA. What?

TESSA. How much?

PATRICIA. My –?

TESSA. Name your price.

PATRICIA. No. No.

(*Beat.*)

I'm not just going to – no, I can't – no, my answer is no.

(**TESSA** *snaps them into Sister Space.*)

**

(*In Sister Space, the air between them is intimate and dangerous.*)

Why did you do that?

TESSA. I just want to talk.

(**PATRICIA** *tries to walk out of Sister Space, but she can't.*)

PATRICIA. Why can't I –

TESSA. Do you really want to be out there with the cameras and not in here with me?

PATRICIA. I –I –

TESSA. I think they're beautiful.

PATRICIA. Well, thank you, but that doesn't change / anything –

TESSA. They're perfect, so sparkling and bright, they're like diamonds.

PATRICIA. Diamonds? I mean, that's very nice but –

TESSA. I think you're beautiful.

(*Beat.*)

PATRICIA. You really think so?

TESSA. I do. You're beautiful.

The way they light up your face, your eyes.

I would cherish them. They would be my most prized possession.

And I wouldn't need many, just a few.

PATRICIA. A few?

TESSA. I'll give you anything you want, anything in the world.

Name your price.

PATRICIA. I dunno, this is crazy –

TESSA. It's not. Most people just don't understand what it takes. But you do, don't you? You're smart. You know what it takes to win.

PATRICIA. It's just too much –

TESSA. It's the last sacrifice you'll <u>ever</u> have to make. Name your price –

PATRICIA. I don't know if I can –

TESSA. You're not very ambitious, are you?

PATRICIA. What?

TESSA. I want one. I can't help it, it's all I can think about.

I want your cheekbones, I want your skin –

PATRICIA. You really want me?

TESSA. I do. I want your hips, I want your lips –

PATRICIA. I want you too.

> (*Inside Sister Space,* **TESSA** *starts: Challenge music.**)

TESSA. I'd only need one. Just let me have one. To remember you by.

> (**PATRICIA** *brings her hand up to her mouth.*)

---

* A license to produce DREAM HOU$E does not include a performance license for any third-party or copyrighted music. Licensees should create an original composition or use music in the public domain. For further information, please see Music Use Note on page 3

PATRICIA. I could try – but it'll cost you.

TESSA. Anything.

PATRICIA. Beg me.

TESSA. Please? For me? Please.

PATRICIA. Is that the best you got? You're not very ambitious, are you?

> (**TESSA** *gets down on her knees to beg.*)

TESSA. Please? Please! Please-please-please, just let me have one, just one – I need it, I know I don't deserve it, I don't deserve you – but you'll be saving my life, I'll owe you my life, please

> (*As* **TESSA** *speaks,* **PATRICIA** *reaches into her mouth and grabs hold of a tooth. She tries to twist it loose, and winces at the pain.*)

> (**TESSA** *reaches into her purse and rummages for something: instead of cash, she takes out a pair of pliers. She offers them to* **PATRICIA**, *who's mesmerized by them.*)

You are going to be so glad you did this. You have so much potential. This is really the investment of a lifetime – and you know, now is a very good time to sell.

> (**PATRICIA** *slowly reaches out to take the pliers.*)

> (*As soon as she touches them,* **TESSA** *immediately pulls them out of Sister Space and back into the show.*)

> (*Note: the pliers should never get near* **PATRICIA**'s *mouth. The moment she touches them is the end of the game.*)

*

(Ding! **PATRICIA** *is exposed to the cameras and the audience again, now with a pair of pliers in her hand.)*

*(***TESSA*** *leaves.* **PATRICIA** *turns to her, but* **TESSA***'s back is already turned.)*

PATRICIA. Wait –

*(***PATRICIA*** *sees the pliers in her hand, and realizes what she's done. She drops the pliers and they land on the floor with a clang. The Challenge music drops out.)*

Did I win?

End of Scene Four

Scene Five

(The **CREW** *comes through like a storm. They add charming midcentury furniture and inoffensive décor to the wreckage of the destroyed walls.)*

*(***TESSA*** *enters, and speaks to the audience with a contented warmth. She's selling the house and in her element.)*

*(***JULIA*** *and* **PATRICIA** *are on either side of her,* **JULIA** *is still holding onto her talismans from the wall.* **PATRICIA** *pulls on professional clothes to cover up her slip.)*

TESSA. Hello! Hello *(Name of producing city!)* and welcome to – say it with me now – *Flip It and List It!*

> *(If the audience doesn't say* Flip It and List It! *Along with* **TESSA**, *she should keep trying until they do.)*

It's time for the open house, and this is the moment of truth for these sisters.

Over a hundred years ago, their ancestors built this house with a dream – a dream of a better life for their family, and for the generations to come. Now, that American Dream could finally come true for these sisters.

They sure have been on a rollercoaster through this process: this old heritage home had more in the walls than they bargained for and the mold infestation was a huge setback. The real estate market in Hi-Vill is booming, but will it be enough to attract a buyer and secure a profit that could take care of the next generation too?

*(**TESSA** addresses the audience like they're a buyer.)*

That's up to you. Follow me, and we can take a tour. I think you're going to absolutely fall in love with this house, I know I sure did. Let's take a look at your new home.

*(**TESSA** leads the imaginary buyer through the home.)*

(The sisters speak to the cameras in the style of a confessional. They're in disconnected spaces and can't hear each other.)

PATRICIA. I'm – I'm back to work again. New clients are coming in.

JULIA. Where am I moving next? I'm looking at places in, um, in Hi-Vill actually.

PATRICIA. They've got a different *level* of expense, and that means more work for me,

JULIA. It's so safe here now, the schools are great, everything's so nice.

PATRICIA. So their pay grade is my pay grade, that's been nice.

JULIA. But moving back to this town –

PATRICIA. But getting all these clients –

JULIA. / It doesn't feel how I thought it would feel –

PATRICIA. It's not what I expected –

(They hear the interruption and there's a pulse of Sister Space.)

**

*

*(They sense it, sense each other. This is the first time they've connected in Sister Space since **TESSA** invaded.)*

*(Then, **TESSA** enters, breaking their eye contact. She's holding a giant novelty check turned backwards to hide the amount.)*

TESSA. Oooooh, guess what?! I've got great news, you're not gonna believe it!

(They sit up a little straighter. Now, they watch each other.)

PATRICIA. They keep calling me 'articulate.' Those new clients, at every consultation. I've gotten that before, but it kept <u>weighing</u> on me and I didn't realize why until –

JULIA. I love the new coffee shop. I love it, and I *hate* that I love it. I love the fair trade blends and the macrame decor. I can't even remember what was there before –

PATRICIA. It hit me how surreal it is that I speak English. It's the only language I really know, the one that I dream in. And not the language of my mother, or her mother, or hers.

JULIA. I got what I wanted right? Me and the baby will have the same hometown, but it's not the same, is it. This isn't the town I left behind. But it is the one I choose to come back to.

PATRICIA. I *was* putting on a voice – and I was proud to do it.

JULIA. *I* want ease, *I* want luxury – and I want it for my daughter too.

(There's a pulse of Sister Space.)

**

*

(*Now the sisters can see each other.*)

(**TESSA** *waits impatiently, eager to tell her news.*)

TESSA. Come on, ladies! You know these outros were really supposed to be more like a 'thanks so much' / to the show.

PATRICIA. It's just like you said. All the blood, the conquest, the violence, the money changing hands – and for what?

JULIA. I can't remember how Mom said my name. Was it Julia? [Julia]? Neither? I just can't hear my name coming from her mouth.

PATRICIA. It's all sitting in the room with me every time I open my mouth. Blood seeps through my teeth, it runs down my chin, and when it does it sounds 'articulate.'

JULIA. [Julia] right? – or – or did she *want* me to be Julia? I lost my mother –

PATRICIA. I lost my mother tongue –

JULIA. Maybe I lost the right to even ask what she called me –

PATRICIA.	**JULIA**.
I ran away.	I ran away.

(*Another Sister Space pulse – it breaks when* **TESSA** *speaks.*)

**

*

(*The sisters move towards each other, speaking over* **TESSA**.)

TESSA. Alright, it's time to wrap it up! –

JULIA. How did Mom say your name? What did she call you?

PATRICIA. With me, she'd just – call out. And I knew she meant me because I was the only one there. She wasn't really calling out for me, just calling out for help.

JULIA. I should've helped, I should've called –

PATRICIA. I miss you –

JULIA. I miss you too –

TESSA. – Don't you want to hear what the house is worth?

> *(The sisters connect physically, finally reaching each other. They snap into Sister Space:)*

> **

> *(And **TESSA** freezes.)*

> *(She doesn't come with them, she stays outside.* ***Sister Space belongs to them again.****)*

> *(They look to **TESSA** and realize that they're alone. They take it in with a deep breath.)*

JULIA. I see what you meant.

I wanted so badly for the past to give me all the answers, but nothing came.

> *(She looks to the Virgin Mary statue.)*

I guess it makes sense. I didn't show up for them, why should they show up for me?

> *(She looks to her sister.)*

I didn't show up for *you.*

I'm so sorry [Pati].

PATRICIA. Thank you.

JULIA. I was just so scared, and I thought she'd get better, and / then when I –

PATRICIA. No, no – you don't have to explain.

JULIA. But I left you to take care of Mom –

PATRICIA. Nobody made me do it. I made a choice.

I'm proud that I was there for her, but there were things I could never say, never be –

And I was hiding behind that. I thought I was getting away with something, pulling off this scheme to get ahead,

(**PATRICIA** *looks to the pliers.*)

But it feels like no matter what I do, no matter what I say, there's just gonna be more blood in my mouth.

(*She has an idea.*)

You know what –

(*Then all of a sudden,* **PATRICIA** *takes up the pliers, goes to the hole in the drywall, and throws them in.*)

(*It's a release.*)

I don't want that anymore – I'm done.

(**JULIA** *looks at the Virgin Mary.*)

JULIA. You're right –

Maybe I should try to just let all this go.

(**JULIA** *turns to the wall, considering throwing the taped-up Virgin Mary inside.*)

PATRICIA. Wait –

> (**PATRICIA** *takes the Mary from* **JULIA**. *She moves toward the hole, but instead of throwing it in, she places the statue on the shelf, in the spot where the altar used to be.*)

Let's rebuild it.

For Mom.

JULIA. For Mom.

> (**JULIA** *and* **PATRICIA** *join together and pick up the items from the wall that are gathered as rubble on the ground.*)

> (*They take the letters, the candle, the family photograph, and the rattle, and arrange them on the shelves in front of the sledgehammer hole in the wall.*)

> (*They re-create the family altar. They take it in.*)

I think we should leave it all here. The letters, the statue, all of it.

PATRICIA. Are you sure?

JULIA. I'm sure. I don't need any of this stuff to honor Mom.

I'll honor her in the way I raise my daughter.

I'll honor her in the way I show up for you.

> (*They take one last look around the house.*)

PATRICIA. I think I'm ready to let go.

JULIA. I am too.

> (**JULIA** *nods. They take a deep breath together, then they embrace.*)

(As they hold each other, the world of the TV show starts to spin back into life in slow motion – **but, JULIA** *and* **PATRICIA** *don't leave Sister Space.)*

(Instead, they stay connected and contained in Sister Space together, even as the cameras roll and the lights blare down on them, even as the **CREW** *winds back up into motion and* **TESSA** *steps forward with the check.)*

(This Sister Space is something new, and more powerful. They can carry it with them anywhere, and it doesn't break for the TV show, for anything.)

*(***TESSA** *is still holding her giant novelty check.)*

TESSA. And now, for the big reveal!

(Dramatic music.*)

We got half a dozen bids and they worked themselves *way* over asking price. This house ended up selling for –

(A drumroll.)

(The sisters do not respond. They're still in Sister Space together, no longer performing for **TESSA** *or the cameras.)*

---

* A license to produce DREAM HOU$E does not include a performance license for any third-party or copyrighted music. Licensees should create an original composition or use music in the public domain. For further information, please see Music Use Note on page 3.

(**TESSA** *flips the novelty check to reveal the amount.*)

Three million dollars!

(**TESSA** *jumps and cheers to celebrate. It's like a one-woman version of the joy explosion in scene one.*)

(*Over speakers: bells and ringing applause. Balloons drop down from the ceiling, confetti falls – incredible spectacle. The* **CREW** *comes on and celebrates too.*)

(*But the sisters pay it no mind. They're peaceful, and focused only on each other.*)

(**TESSA** *doesn't understand why they aren't jumping for joy.*)

Congratulations – we did it! How do you feel!?

(*The sisters don't answer her.*)

Come on, isn't this amazing! Aren't you happy? I mean holy heck it's three million dollars, that's so much more than we thought this place could ever be worth!

(*No response.*)

I promised you I'd get the best price I possibly could, and I did! I did what you wanted! I got what you deserve! Didn't I?

Aren't you happy?

… Aren't you happy?!

(*The sisters look to the check, and then to each other.*)

(*Blackout.*)

End of Play